Loch Warriors

1

Corey Lloyd

Contents

Prologue
Chapter 1 – Kori
Chapter 2 – Loch Warrior exam
Chapter 3 – Team Izanagi
Chapter 4 – First Mission
Chapter 5 – The others
Chapter 6 – Looner
Chapter 7 – Looner Vs Enji
Chapter 8 – Brume Tower
Chapter 9 – Level two
Chapter 10 – Soul Witch
Chapter 11 – Lightening vs Sound
Chapter 12 - Absolute
Chapter 13 – Success
Chapter 14 – Namiyo
Chapter 15 – Preparation
Chapter 16 – Round one
Chapter 17 – Drakai vs Tenkai
Chapter 18 – Rain
Chapter 19 – War announcement

Prologue

Loch is a huge country, located on the left side of Asros and Nortdrum it's neighbouring countries. All three were one land over eight hundred years ago but a war between gods occurred. Olette the fairy god tried to defend her home from Okifumi, his evil intent drove chaos through the lands. The war brewed on, but there was one man who would put a stop to this war, his name was Malek, he became a Loch Warrior, he said the Loch Warrior is to protect the planet from evil like Okifumi.

They both had an intense battle, Okifumi was finally defeated and Malek was victorious but the country was split into three and Malek was gravely injured. Olette vanished after she thanked Malek for saving everyone. After Malek passed, the left country was named Loch and the king commanded that every magic user to follow in the footsteps of Malek, in which the order of the Loch Warriors was in full effect.

Many, many years later, Nortdrum had a dark secret, the dark kingdom would secretly take over and plot the destruction of Loch, this war between Loch and the dark kingdom would go on for a very long time, but the Loch Warrior would always be victorious. The dark kingdoms motives would still be unknown, the king thinks they must want land from Loch but has said there is a darker secret and that the Loch Warriors will not rest and that the Dark kingdom will fall.

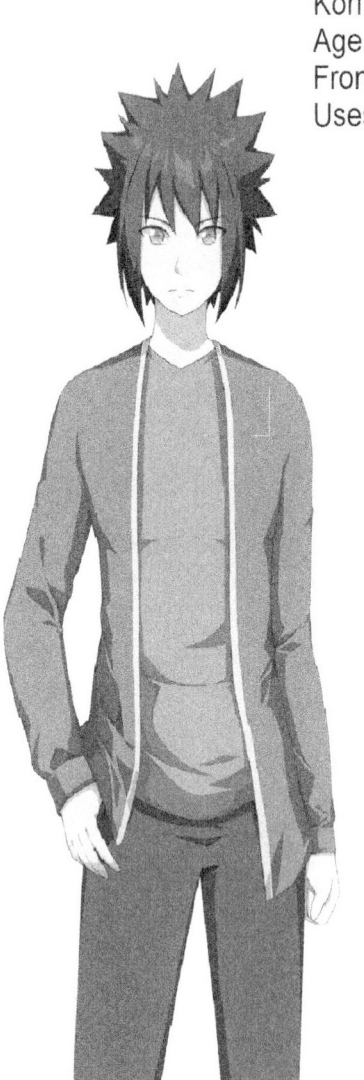

Kori Tenkai
Age 15
From Kingfish Village
Uses Wood Magic

1 - Kori

Kingfish village was blooming with life as it is that time of the year for fishermen to fish in the docks, Kori Tenkai a fifteen-year-old boy watches from the top of the highest hill.

"Man, I hope I pass the ritual tomorrow" he thought.

"Kori, Kori!!" someone shouted behind him. Kori turns, and sees a guy running towards him in the distance, he squints his eyes and sees that it is his friend Daichi.

"What is it Daichi?".

"Master Shin wants to see you in the dojo".

"Oh, you did not have to run, I am sure the old man wants to give me some words of wisdom for tomorrow".

"True, I can't believe you are going to go to Loch Warrior Academy, I hear Master Shin is a grade 3 Loch Warrior, one of the highest ranks".

"The highest rank is Head Loch Warrior, that is my goal, to become the strongest Loch Warrior, but I still have to pass the ritual tomorrow".

"Well I am sure you will pass; your magic is strong and if anyone can achieve their dream it is you, good luck" said Daichi.

"Thanks, I will do my best".

Kori heads through the village, everyone greets him and wishes him luck for tomorrow, he appreciates everyone's kind words, he walks up a steep hill and sees Master Shin's dojo. He slides open the wooden door and sees the room is dark but lit up at the back with candles.

"Ah, Kori, come on in" said Master Shin, he stands near a black alter.

Kori walks up to him and sees he is meditating, "what's up old man Shin?".

"Old man, I see you are respectful as ever, listen tomorrow is your ritual, if you pass you will be accepted into the Loch Warrior Academy as a Loch Warrior in training, before that I must see your magical energy".

Kori powers his magic, the aura glows around him, Master Shin is impressed as always by Kori's magical energy.

"Very good, your power is decent, the ritual will be a success tomorrow, so make sure you get a good night's sleep".

"Okay will do Master, right I best be off, see you later".
Kori leaves the dojo to head back to his small home, he lives alone inside the village, he never knew his parents as he was dropped off at Kingfish village when he was a baby, he was taken in by Master Shin and grew up with the village.

Kori makes some smoked salmon and eats at his small table by himself, after he eats this delicacy and heads straight to bed ready for the Loch Warrior ritual tomorrow morning. As he begins to drift off, a commotion can be heard from outside. He sits up and wipes his eyes, he looks out the window and is stunned to see building up in flames.

"What the hell?".

He jumps out of bed and changes into his clothes, he opens the door and hears screams from all over the village.

Kori runs into the village centre and sees people being attacked by men in black robes, they were using steel swords to slaughter people. Kori quickly acts and uses wood magic to tie vines around the arms of these men, he then controls the vines and slams them hard onto the solid floor. A man appears behind him and swings his sword fast; Kori sees this coming and ducks as the sword is swung above his head, he turns and roundhouse kicks the man in the side of the head, knocking him out completely. Kori looks up the hill and sees Master Shin and others taking on these hooded men, but suddenly he could hear a fight down below into the market area.

"Master Shin is a powerful Loch Warrior, he can handle this area, I will go and help down the road" Kori thought.

He enters the market area and sees people dead; this makes him angry as he sees the hooded men laughing surrounding someone.

"Oi, challenge me you scum!!" Kori shouted. The men turn around, one of them is holding a battered Daichi, this makes Kori see red, he uses his wood magic to create huge tree stems shoot from the ground whacking a couple of them into the nearby buildings. The man holding Daichi is afraid and holds Daichi at knife point, pressing a small dagger to his throat.

"Do not move kid, I will cut his throat".

"Let him go now" Kori said.

A huge muscular man teleports behind Kori, Kori is shocked as he turns his head, the man smashes Kori into the ground with super speed.

"Kori!!" Daichi shouted.

The man holding Daichi laughs and throws him to the floor, he draws a blade and is ready to stab Daichi, but Daichi kicks the man in the gut and grabs a wooden plank and begins to beat the man by bashing him on the head. A few more hooded men appear and knock Daichi to the ground. Kori looks up and sees one of them drive their steel sword straight through Daichi's chest.

"Ha, that's what he gets for standing up to the dark kingdom, idiot" said the man with huge muscles.

Kori grips the dirt and his pupils begin to glow red, the aura around Kori becomes immense as his magical energy begins to smother everyone. He uses a new move and shoots huge wooden stakes out of the ground, impaling every single hooded man. Blood rains down upon Kori, covering him and his clothes in blood. Kori's eyes turn back to green as he falls unconscious from using such magical power.

The sun was bright, Kori opens his eyes and sees the glorious blue ocean, he turns and sees Daichi, but he was much younger.

"Where am I?" Kori asked.

"You are just dreaming Kori, but this is one of our best memories, look how peaceful it is, such simpler times" said Daichi.

"Oh yeah, this is the place we first met, you wanted to board a ship and sail across that ocean and I told you that I wanted to become a Loch Warrior".

"Yeah, it is a shame I will never see what is across that ocean" said Daichi.

"Huh, but you are not dead just yet, I will save you".

"I appreciate it Kori, but my time is up, but do not be sad, you will have to live both of our dreams, so do not let me down".

Kori eventually comes too and opens his eyes, the rain falls down on him, he sits up and sees Master Shin and the villagers checking on people. Kori turns his head and sees Daichi lying in the dirt, he walks over to him and looks down with sorrow.

"I am sorry my friend".

Daichi coughs and Kori is shocked to see him still alive, he kneels down to check on him.

"Daichi can you hear me?".

"Don't apologies, I did this to protect the village, I am proud of what I did and especially proud of you for stopping every one of them".

"We can still heal you; I am sure you will survive".

"No, my wound is fatal, I think I only have a few minutes left, so do not feel sad".

Kori's eyes begin to water knowing he cannot do anything to help his friend, Daichi uses the last of his strength to put his hand on Kori's shoulder.

"Promise me, you will follow your dream and live your life to the full, I know you will become the strongest Loch Warrior".

"I promise".

Daichi passes away, the rest of the morning the villagers bury the dead and hold a service for everyone, Kori and other members of the dojo help rebuild what was destroyed in the fires. Nightfall arrives and Kori heads inside the dojo to see Master Shin.

"You ready kid?" he said.

"Yeah, let's do this".

"Ah he has a fire in his eye that I have not seen before" Master Shin thought.

Master Shin pulls out a golden dagger, he holds it carefully and looks Kori in the eyes, "this is the dagger of Merrick the first Loch Warrior, cut yourself and drop blood into the dish on top of the alter, inside the dish is Merrick's blood, fusing the two bloods will bound you to being a Loch Warrior" he explained.

Kori takes the dagger, he looks nervous as he slices his hand, he places his hand over the dish and blood drops into the dish, he steps back and waits. "What now Master?" Kori asked.

"Wait and see young man".

The dish begins to glow, and magical energy begins building within the alter, suddenly a beam of light shoots up and out of the dish into the hole in the roof. The light was blinding, and the magic felt from the light was powerful. A shadow appears in the middle of the light, Kori felt something from this as he goes in to grab it, he pulls it out of the light and sees that it is a medallion with a yellow upward arrow. The light fades away and Kori is left looking confused, he looks to Master Shin for answers.

"The medallion means the ritual was a success, this is a Loch Warrior pass that you will need to be identified as a Loch Warrior".

"It looks so cool".

"Right listen Kori, you need to head to Loch Kingdom to the academy, there you will spend three years learning and working as a Loch Warrior in training".

"I have to go to Loch Kingdom, where is that?" Kori scratches his head in confusion.

"It is okay, I will arrange a horse and carriage to take you down there".

"Ah, thank you master, I will go and pack my things".

Kori heads out to go to his shack to pack what things he has in there. Master Shin smiles knowing that Kori will do well as a Loch Warrior.

Before Kori heads to meet Master Shin, he heads to the grave of his friend Daichi.

"Daichi, watch down over me, I will fulfil my promise to you, thank you for being a great friend".

Kori bids him farewell and travels to the edge of the village to meet up with Master Shin who waits beside a horse and carriage.

"Well Kori, good luck to you, make sure you look after yourself, the kingdom can be a very dangerous place".

"I will thank you Master I will not let you down".

Kori boards the carriage and waves back at Master Shin as he heads down the long road, he travels South East to Loch Kingdom a long five-day journey.

2 – Loch warrior Exam

Loch Kingdom is located Southeast in Loch, it is next to the coast, a huge kingdom with tall buildings and on top of a great hill was the castle in which the King would rule from. On the boarder of the fortress that surrounds the great city is the Loch Warrior headquarters. A building surrounded by tall trees and a huge path leading towards it.

Outside the Loch Academy fellow Loch Warriors in training begin to arrive, Kori travels down in his carriage. He gets of the carriage and thanks the driver for taking him all this way. He then walks down the stone path leading to the building. He sees all the people walking to the building and smiles as he senses their magical energy and knows each one of them are strong.

"I can't wait to see what magic these guys use" He thought.

"Hey there…" someone said behind Kori. Kori turns to see who it was and sees a guy with red hair and yellow eyes wearing a white shirt with a black tie.

"Hi" Kori awkwardly said.

"I am Drake Xero; I sensed your magical energy and can tell you are strong".

"Thanks, I am Kori Tenkai".

"You see, everyone here is a bit full of themselves but me, I like to find people who are pure and want to be friendly".

"Oh right, well I guess I am quite friendly".

"See, let's be friends".

"Sure, I guess we can be friends, so do you know where I am going, I am quite lost".

"Your lost, but the Academy is right there, we are meant to all gather in the hall and await the Head Loch Warrior's presentation".

"Head Loch Warrior I am excited".

"Yeah, he is the leader and the strongest Loch Warrior, he will tell us our path that we will take from here on out".

"I see, well let's get going Drake".
They both head into the academy and make their way into the grand hall, a huge open space with seats and a large wooden stage. They both sit next to each other and look around and see a lot of nervous faces.

"Hey Drake, why does everyone look nervous?" Kori whispered.

"You may have done the ritual, but there is a huge test we must do before being accepted into the academy, those who do not pass have to wait a whole year before being allowed to enter again".

"WHAT!! A TEST!!" Kori shouts, people turn their heads to look who shouted, Kori embarrassed looks to the ground.

"Yeah, a test, please don't shout people will think we are disrespecting them and will probably target us, but the test is random every year so no one knows what sort of test it could be, but if you are confident in your abilities then there should be nothing to worry about".

Kori looks around again and sees a death stare from a huge guy with spiky white hair, his blue eyes stared into Kori's eyes which creeped Kori out.

"Jeez what's his deal?" Kori asked.

"That's Drake Drakai, he is a ice magic user, he comes from a powerful family, he probably doesn't like you because of the Tenkai and Drakai feud from way before we were born".

"Family feud, I have no idea who my family are so we should just make up and become good friends".

"Ha ha sure".

The stage lights up, everyone peels their eyes forward as a grey-haired man with a thick beard walks onto the stage.

"Welcome to all, I am Ichiro Kido, I am the head of the Loch Warriors, I hope everyone's journey here was good but today is the start of your lives, Loch Warriors are prestige magic users who use their magic to help others, over the next three years you will be based in four man squads reporting to a Grand Loch Warrior, but before I place each one of you in your squads you must pass a test".

"Okay, here we go, I have to be better than the competition, I cannot go back to Kingfish

Village without fulfilling my promise" Kori thought.

"The test will be a practical, group up in threes and go to the booth outside, the paper will be given to you to tell you the location to head to for your test, so good luck everyone and remember Loch Warrior's work in teams".

"So, we need to be in a group of three?" Kori asked.

"Yeah, lets you and I team up, we just need to find one more person then".

"Yeah, I am down for that".

Kori and Drake wait outside the academy asking people to join their group but everyone they asked so far declined.

"Oh man, this is so hard, do people think we are losers or something?" Drake wondered.

"Most likely, we aren't the tallest of people, but that's life, people underestimate the small guys" Kori said.

A shy girl with short blue hair stands beside a tree looking nervous.

"She is the only person left, but with our magical abilities we could pass just using our magic".

Kori walks over to her and startles her; she hides behind the tree.

"Hey there, I am Kori Tenkai, and I will become the strongest Loch Warrior, I would like it if you joined my team for the test".

"Erm, s-sure, but why me, if you are to be the strongest why ask a weakling like me to join, what if you fail the test".

"I will not fail, and you are not weak, I can sense magical aura and your magical energy is very strong so please join".

She blushes at Kori's words, "okay I will join, my name is Luna Evergrande".

"That's a nice name, welcome to the team Luna".

Everyone heads to the five stations outside the academy to collect their mission tickets for their test. Drake heads to the station first and is given a piece of red envelope, he takes this to Kori and Luna, and he opens it.

"Looks like co-ordinates, they seem to be a mile into the forest" Drake explains.

"Sweet, let's go and do the test guys," said Kori.

The three head deep into the forest, finally getting to the right co-ordinates. They seem a little confused as no one is here.

"This is a bit strange, no proctor to test us and nothing but trees around us," said Drake.

"I sense someone heading this way," said Luna.

"She's right, the magical energy is huge, it's coming from behind us," said Kori.

They all turn around nervous as a huge magical energy approaches. From the trees a thing speeds past and a loud thud can be heard behind them. They turn and see a man with a long red jacket and brown hair.

"Why hello their kids," said the man.

"Who are you?" Drake asked.

"My name is Atticus, I am a Grand Loch Warrior, I am here to test you guys".

"Wow a Grand Loch Warrior, so cool" Kori excitingly said.

"That's correct spiky boy, now listen up, the test is simple, a mile north is a Monster, defeat it".

"Is that it, this should be a breeze," said Kori.

"That's it, good luck, the monster is big so you can't really miss it".

The three rushes into the forest to get the test underway, Kori heads to the top of the tree just to see if he is able to spot it from up high.

"Hmm, where could it be?" he looks around scratching his head while holding onto the highest branch, "oh wait, I see a shiny metal thing moving could that be it?".

He jumps down the tree and informs the others of what he has found, they head in that direction to confront what it is that he saw.

Kori, Luna, and Drake sneak through the bushes getting a peak at what they could be facing.

"Is that a metallic bull?" Luna asked.

"Yeah, it has the number 7 printed onto it's right leg, which means the other teams are probably facing something similar" Drake explained.

"Well don't mind me, I will take this bull out easy," said Kori.

He flies out of the bushes and jumps in front of the metallic bull.

"You are mine" Kori said as he points straight at the bull.

The Bull stamps onto the floor causing the ground to shake, it charges fast towards Kori. It puts its sharp horns down while charging, Kori jumps over the bull and lands behind it. He places his hands on the ground and uses wood magic to wrap wooden vines around its legs to keep it in place.

"Very smart, keeping it still, what will he do next?" Drake thought.

Kori smiles giving the thumbs up to Luna and Drake, the bull easily rips the vines out of the ground as he jumps back and goes to hit Kori with a back kick, Kori puts his arms covering his face and chest as the kick connects knocking him into a nearby tree.

"Damn!!, come Luna, lets help him," said Drake.

They come out of the bushes as Drake throws a fire ball at the bull distracting it as Luna runs over to Kori to check on him.

"Are you okay?" Luna asked.

"Yeah, the bull is stronger than I thought" said Kori, he sits up and watches on as Drake fights the bull.

The bull thrusts it's horns but Drake dodges and lands a fire ball on the left back leg of the bull causing the bull to kneel. Kori gets up and uses his wood magic to create vines once more, but the vines are much stronger and thicker. Luna washes off being nervous and shows her magic. She uses spirit magic to create a medium sizes jelly fish covered in blue aura, she shoots this at the bull causing a huge explosion.

"Wow, your magic is awesome Luna," said Kori.

"Thank you, it's my spirit magic".

"Nice guys, I think we got it" Drake said. The smoke eventually clears, and the Bull's eyes went from yellow to red, Drake is shocked as he stands and begins unloading fire balls at the Bull.

"This test is hard, how are we meant to beat a Bull that can't be defeated?" Luna wondered.

"There may be a way, here" Kori began whispering in Luna's ear.

Kori walks up to the Bull and uses wood magic to create a vine that he grabs with his hand, the Bull is aggressive and begins chasing Kori, Kori evades and begins running around the Bull's legs wrapping the long vine around.

Luna runs over to Drake, "here is the plan, Kori is going to wrap the vine around it's legs, we then unleash our magic and knock it onto it's back so it cannot move" she explained to him.

"That's a good plan, if we cannot destroy it, we incapacitate it" Drake thought.

Drake uses fire magic to light up his hand in flames, he calls this magic Fire Fist, he darts at the Bull and punches it on the side tipping the bull almost sideways. Luna quickly uses Soul magic and fires a Soul Jellyfish towards the spot Drake hit, it explodes as a white and blue sparkle knocking the Bull on its back.

"Nice guys" said Kori, he tightens the vines so it can't move its legs.

Kori turns his head back as he sees Atticus come from the bushes clapping his hands.

"Well done guys' you pass" he said with a smile.

"Yes!!" Kori shouted.

"At first you guys were just attacking the Bull on your own, but when you become a team, you worked well and came up with a plan that would stop the Bull so congratulations".

"Wait so you were watching us all along?" Drake asked.

"Well, I am your examiner but do remember you three may not work together again, as later on in the evening you will be placed into a group of four people with a sensei who is a Grand Loch Warrior".

"Awe, that sucks, well Luna and Drake good luck and I hope we do end up in the same group but with the amount of people here the chances do not seem to be good," said Kori.

"Yeah, don't worry Kori, whoever we have in our team we need to remember teamwork is key like Mr Atticus told us" said Drake.

"Let's head back guys, if we are late then we may not even get put into a group" Luna nervously said.

3 – Team Izanagi

The exams are over, and everyone heads to the main hall to await instruction from the Head Loch Warrior. Only twelve people passed the exam, Kori was shocked by how many people failed.

"Wow Drake can you believe how many people failed?".

"This is natural Kori; the others must have failed to work as a team and failed to beat whatever they had to take out" Drake explained.

Kori turns and sees that huge man with white hair glaring at him.

"That strange guy again, David is his name..." Kori thought.

The room went quite as Ichiro walks onto the stage; he looks over to the first years with a warm smile on his face.

"Congratulations on passing the exam, you twelve will now be sorted into teams of four, you will work with each other over the next three years, after which you will become full fledge Loch Warriors" he explained.

Kori smiles as he feels proud from Master Ichiro's words.

"Now, one of my magical abilities is mind magic, I will tell you about a number in your head, you then head to that door number in the academy, this will be your base and for you to meet your team-mates and sensei".

"Mind magic?" Kori asked confusingly.

"This is a rare magic, telepathy," said Drake.

"Five" Kori heard in his head.

"Incredible, I heard his voice clear as day, so five is the door I must go" Kori thought.

Everyone begins leaving the hall, Kori wishes Drake good luck as the two shake hands and head their separate ways. Kori wonders down the long hallway, he seemed lost and begins to panic.

"Oh no, how am I at door thirty-nine, where is five? Oh no oh no" he muttered.

He wonders around the corner and bumps into a tall man, he falls on his butt and looks up in shock.

"Hey, it's tall lanky man," said Kori.

"First of all, my name is David Drakai, you are that Tenkai boy" he said, glaring his blue eyes at Kori.

"So, what if we have similar last names, you have a weird spiky white hair cut".

"Wrong, my hair is in fashion".

"Right, can you tell me where door number five is please?".

"No, only if you tell me where door number sixteen is?".

"Ha so you are lost too, not so smart for a giant".

"Midget, door number five was near the beginning of the hallway".

"I knew that" said Kori as he stands and runs down the hall.

"What's his problem?" Kori thought.

Finally, Kori arrives at the door, it had five in huge letters, he shrugs as he opens the door and sees Luna standing with two guys.

"Oh, hey Luna, so you are on my team?".

"Yeah, the old master said five in my head".

"Oh cool, glad I see a familiar face, hi all, I am Kori Tenkai, and I am going to be the strongest Loch Warrior".

"Loser" said the boy with brown spiky hair, he turns his head with his eyes closed.

"Wow the strongest, but you are only two feet tall" said the boy with blond spiky hair.

"Hey, I am five foot four, and who you are calling a loser hedgehog guy".

"There is no way you will be the strongest, I can sense your magic, you are nothing special, seem to know we are introducing ourselves, I am Silva Mainz".

"Oh cool, I am Kaito Mizuno".

"Erm, I am Luna Evergrande".

"Very good now I don't have to do ice breakers" everyone turns to the door to see who said that.

A man with a white and gold cloak stands behind Kori, his hair was blond and very spiky, he throws up the peace sign and smiles.

"I am your sensei, but you can call me Master Izanagi".

"This is our teacher, he's worse than that loud kid" Silva thought.

"Wow, this guy is amazing, his cloak, his hair and his manly voice" Kori thought.

He walks over to the white board and turns to everyone; he points for them to take their seats.

"Okay everyone, we will do introductions again, but this time I want to know why you want to be a Loch Warrior".

He points to Luna, "you go first blue haired girl".

"Er, right sensei, I am Luna Evergrande and I want to be a Loch Warrior just like my mother was".

"Evergrande, I see Evelyn Evergrande, she was a very strong magic user, up next you".

"I am Kaito Mizuno, I wanted to become a Loch Warrior so I can make my family proud".

"Strange one, erm you".

"I am Silva Mainz, I wanted to be a Loch Warrior so I can gain power that would allow me to follow my true path".

"Dark, I kinda dig that, last one".

"I am Kori Tenkai, I wanted to be a Loch Warrior so I can be the strongest Loch Warrior, so I can fulfil a promise I made to my friend and my village, I will not give up until I achieve everyone's respect".

"I see, you all have your own aspirations, I do not judge on your goals, I am Izanagi Sasaki, I am currently the strongest Grand Loch Warrior, my goal is to one day retire on a large farm".

Everyone looked shocked, "see everyone has a dream or a goal, so support each other on your goal's, we have three years to make you into solid Loch Warrior's".

"Yes sensei," said Kori.

"Good, good, now listen up all, we have a big day tomorrow, so for now head to your chambers, your name will be on the door, the girls' chambers are located on the right wing the boys on the left, food will be served in the main hall three points in the day and yeah be prepared" Izanagi explained, he teleports away.

"Wow he just vanished, incredible," said Kori.

"So annoying" said Silva as he walks out the room.

"Come Kori, let's go find our rooms, Luna we will see you at main hall for dinner" said Kaito.

The two run off down the halls and up the stairs, they find their rooms and are excited to see what's inside. Kori opens his and sees a small room with a bed and a chair and desk.

"Wow, it's bigger than where I lived in Kingfish village cool".

Kori looked out the window and sees the sun set on the academy, he smiles and remembers his friend Daichi, he feels his destiny is running full force.

"Now this is where my new adventure begins, time to show everyone my wonderful magic" he thought as he smiles.

Silva Mainz

4 – First Mission

The morning after and everyone has settled in, Kori and his team meet up outside the academy to wait for Izanagi.

"So early in the morning" said Kori, he yawned.

"It is, where is Master Izanagi?" Kaito asked.

"Behind you all".

Everyone turns and sees Izanagi waving from the side of a tree with the cheekiest grin.

"Master why did you want us all to meet here?" Silva asked.

"I am here to deliver your first mission" he said.

"Yes, finally a mission I cannot wait" Kori jumps with joy.

"A mission?" Silva wondered.

"You are to travel to Chisana village, there has been members of the dark kingdom there, find out information and if you run into them, then take them down, if we can capture them, it would be big for us".

"Dark Kingdom, the ones who attacked King Fish village" Kori thought.

"Master, are you not going to be there with us?" Luna asked.

"Good question Luna, I have a mission of my own, once I have done that I will be with you guys, but remember if things get two dangerous you must retreat until I get there, that is why I am making Silva team captain, his ability to sense magical energy will tell you if an opponent is too strong".

"Awe, this guy team captain," said Kori.

"Right, everyone start going, Kaito here is a map, you should be there within six hours".

Izanagi teleports away, Kori and the team begin to set off down the road, Kaito directs them to head East to where the village is.

"So, Kori what is your magic type?" Kaito asked.

"I use wood magic, bout yourself?"

"Lightening magic, I have adapted to quite a few techniques".

"Decent, Silva what magic do you use?".

"Wind magic" he said.

"Wind magic is cool, Luna?".

"Spirit magic, I don't fully understand it, but I can create explosive jellyfish's".

"Hey explosive Jellyfish sounds amazing; I cannot wait to see it" said Kaito.

Silva stops as he looks concerned, Luna realises, "What's wrong Silva?".

"I sense the dark kingdom".

Everyone freezes and looks around; Kori tries to sense but cannot really sense anything.

"It must be coming from the village, but I sense a few magical energies and one that is huge".

"I wonder if the huge one is a leader of some sort" Kori thought.

"Let's keep going we should be there soon; we will just have to be careful when we enter the village" said Silva.

After an few more hours of walking they come to the end of the road and spot the village in the distance, a few buildings with a lake on the left side. Silva leads the team right; they walk below a small hill near the buildings.

"Silva, can you sense where in the village they are?" Kaito asked.

"The huge magical energy is to the far back of the village, smaller energies are in the centre of the village".

"Right, I am a sneaky boy, so I will sneak around the buildings, I can mask my magical energy," said Kori.

"He's right, I cannot sense anything from him," said Silva.

"Good idea Kori" said Kaito.

"Be careful though," said Luna.

"Do not worry, if things get dangerous, I will raise my magical energy".

Kori runs up the hill and shimmers between the buildings. He spots men in cloaks leading villagers into an underground area.

"They must be keeping the villager's hostage, bastards" Kori thought.

He looks left and sees a man with a cloak asleep on a wooden chair. He smiles as places his hand on the dirt, he shoots a small vine from the ground to choke the man, knocking him unconscious. He sneaks over and takes the cloak of the guy and wears it himself. He places the man inside the building and begins to walk the village centre.

"Hopefully they don't suspect me".
The cloaks hood hides the top part of Kori's face, he walks around and sees that there is only seven men with cloaks, he remembers what Silva told him.

"The strongest one is at the back, I wanna check him out".

He walks past two cloaked men and spots a man meditating at the tallest building at the back of the village.

"That's him, I can sense his magical energy now".

The meditating man was not wearing a cloak, he had long black hair and wore no shirt, his muscles are massive. The man opens his eyes and looks directly at Kori.

"Crap".
Kori turns and begins to slowly walk away; the meditating man stands.

"You there" he said.

"Yeah" said Kori as he turns to the man.

"Find me some wine in this disgusting village" he said.

"Yes sir, will do".

"Damn that was close, I felt his stare piercing right through me" Kori thought as he wipes the sweat of his forehead.

He hears a commotion to the right near the tunnel. He sees a cloaked man knock over an elderly man.

"Stupid old man, know your place," said the cloaked man.

He punches the man in the face and pulls out a sword.

"Damn I need to do something" Kori thought.

He points the sword at the old man, the villagers are all worried as the clocked man is about to kill him.

Kori quickly places his hand on the floor and launches a huge log at full speed smashing the cloaked man in the back sending him crashing into the lake.

"What..." the cloaked men are all confused. Kori tears the cloak of himself, his face is full of rage.

"You bunch of cowards attacking a defenceless village, I will destroy you all" Kori said.

Silva senses Kori's magic, he looks up wondering what is going on.

"Let's go guys, Kori is fighting".

The man at the back walks towards Kori smiling.

"Wood magic, that is a good magical ability boy, I am Akio, the commander of the third squad".

"I am Kori Tenkai, a Loch Warrior".

"Well Kori Tenkai, let's see you handle my men" said Akio, he turns to his men, five of them and nods for them to attack.

Kori readies himself, two of them run forward to tag team Kori, but are blown away by a high wind attack. Kori turns and sees Silva, Kaito and Luna run up behind him.

"You good?" Kaito asked.

"Yeah, I had no choice they was about to kill a villager".

"It's okay, we would have done the same thing, as a loch warrior it is our absolute priority to protect people" said Kaito.

"Right, the problem is that big guy over there, Kori you and I will take him, Kaito and Luna you guys take the remaining three in front of us" Silva instructs.

"Right!!" everyone said.

Kori and Silva walk up to Akio, he has his arms folded and smirks at them.

"Four young loch warriors, how good is this, I will kill all of you and throw the loch warriors into a mess".

"Kill us, how pitiful, we will defeat you here and capture you," said Silva.

"Damn, I am just bluffing here, there is no way me and Kori beat this guy, his magical power is off the chart, we cannot run as I am sure he could catch us in an instant, we just have to by time for Master Izanagi to arrive" Silva thought.

Silva uses wind magic to send a wave of high winds at Akio, he brushes this off with a swipe of one hand which shocks Silva. Kori rushes in and strikes Akio with a right punch which is blocked by his right hand.

"You have some power kid, shame your potential is going to be wasted".

He grabs Kori's hand and hammers him to the ground with his left fist, Silva appears above him and uses tornado wind to strike the ground below. This creates a dust cloud, he looks on in the sky as it clears, he sees that Akio is not there.

"Behind you..." a mutter behind Silva. He turns and sees he is in the air behind him, Akio kicks Silva sending him crashing into the ground. He lands and sees vines speeding towards him, he smiles as he lets the vines wrap around his arms and chest to suppress him.

"Silva, NOW!!" Kori shouts.

Silva uses Wind Cannon and blasts Akio direct; this destroys the building behind him.

"Yes, got him" said Kori.

The dust clears and Akio is stood disappointed as he just looks up to the sky.

"So weak" he said.

"Damn, nothing we do affects this guy, we need Luna and Kaito" he turns and sees they are fighting the last cloaked man.

He pulls off his cloak revealing himself, he has blond hair with green eyes.

"You may have got past the weaklings I call team-mates, but I am Jinzo, second in command to Lord Akio's squad".

"Who cares your still a scumbag" said Kaito.

"Scumbag, how dare you call me that you little rat".

Kaito uses lightening magic to amplify his speed, he teleports behind Jinzo and uses lightening elbow to knock him forward, Luna quickly releases a Spirit jellyfish, she sends it directly at him. Jinzo sees this and flips over the Jellyfish and rushes towards Luna. Luna freezes not knowing what to do, Jinzo pulls out a knife and goes for the stab.

Blood drips onto the ground, Jinzo is shocked, Kaito blocked the knife with the palm of his hand.

"You are one quick boy," said Jinzo.

Lightening begins to radiate from Kaito's body, he looks to Jinzo with rage in his eyes.

"I called you a scumbag because you are one, you attacked a girl with a sharp object, not even using your magic, what a disgrace" said Kaito.

Kaito charges his magical energy to create a technique called Inazuma-dama, a yellow and white orb appears in his right hand, Jinzo begins to sweat as Kaito launches the orb into Jinzo's chest launching him into the sky, the orb explodes causing a huge electrical explosion. Jinzo crashes into the lake and is defeated.

"Wow nice move Kaito," said Kori.

"That guy has decent magic, but there is no way he can create more, his magical energy is almost exhausted" Akio thought.

Kaito and Luna stand beside Kori and Silva, Kaito pulls out the knife from his palm and throws it to the floor.

"You ready guys, well team Izanagi!!" said Kori.

"Yeah" everyone said.

"Well, very good for beating all my men but you have no chance in beating me," said Akio.

"This energy, he's close, we just have to hold him off" Silva thought.

Kaito release a lightning strike towards Akio, he dodge but is hit by a wind cannon from Silva, Akio falls down and dodges a jelly fish bomb from Luna. Kori quickly appears behind Akio and kicks him in the face, cutting the bottom lip of Akio.

"Well, you drew some blood, well done," said Akio.

He back elbow's Kori in the face, knocking him to the ground, then he quickly sprints at Kaito and releases his magic. His hands turn to steel grey and jabs Kaito in the ribs then hammers him to the ground. Silva shocked releases a small tornado to try and swoop Akio into the sky while Luna charges up another Jellyfish. Akio smirks as he releases huge amount of magical energy to destroy the tornado, he raises his hand and metal poles shoot from the ground smashing into the chests of Luna and Silva, they fall to the ground in pain.

"See, you are all weak, how the Loch Warriors have fallen, pitiful".

Kori looks up and sees his comrades have fallen, he punches the ground in frustration.

"I am so weak; I cannot even protect my new team-mates" Kori said.

"You are weak, use my magical energy and you will win".

"Who was that a voice in my head, I must be going crazy" Kori said.

"You won last time with my magic, now agree and use my magic, blood magic".

"Fine, whoever you are give me your energy," said Kori.

Akio stands above Silva, he lifts his foot up and is about to stomp on him, but he stops as he feels huge magical energy behind him. He turns and sees a red and black aura surround Kori.

"What is this?" Akio asked.

Kori looks up and his eyes glow red, he has rage on his face as his magical energy is out of control.

Kori teleports in front of Akio and smashes him in the gut, Akio backs up and coughs up blood. Kori sees this and uses blood magic; he makes the blood Akio coughed up explode knocking Akio into a nearby wooden shack.

"How has he gotten so strong and how can he control blood?" Silva wondered.

Kori laughs, he points to Akio as he stands up, "you are very weak peasant".

"What did you say you little brat," said Akio.

Akio turns his full body into steel, creating a greater defence. He begins to run at Kori, quickly thought Kori uses black tree magic and covers Akio's legs in tree branches, Akio tries to punch the tree branches, but they wouldn't snap or break.

"You cannot break this magic, now for my special move," said Kori.

Kori picks up the dagger and cuts down his arm drawing blood, he uses lightening magic infused with blood magic to create red lightening.

"Kori can use lightening magic?" Kaito was shocked.

"How the hell has he got so much magical types, what monster is he?" Akio asked.

Kori teleports in front of Akio and fires his red lightening upon him causing a massive explosion. The shock wave blew a few trees out of the ground. The smoke cloud was huge, it was hard to see for Silva and the others as they hope Kori defeated Akio. The cloud clears and Kori is breathing heavy as his eyes turn back to green. Akio stands in the crater, his steel magic worn off as his magical energy is exhausted due to protecting himself from that attack.

"Damn what power that kid has, good thing my steel protects me from the lightening, but the blood infused with it makes that attack more dangerous, but it looks like both our magical energies are drained, but I have strength on my side" Akio thought.

He jumps and lands behind Kori, Silva sees that Kori is out of it and tries to pull himself up to help him.

"It's over boy, good effort though," said Akio.

Akio freezes as he senses a huge magical power appear a few meters behind him. He turns and sees a man with a golden cloak with huge spiky hair.

"Master Izanagi" said Silva.

"You all did well, now let me take over," said Izanagi.

"Who the hell are you?" Akio asked.

"Izanagi, Grand Loch Warrior, I shall take you out in one simple move".

"Grand Loch Warrior, one move he is bluffing, I still have a bit of magic, if I use my steel defence and block his attack I can counter with a devastating right hook, perfect" he thought.

He looks up and Izanagi has vanished, he is shocked and looks around but does not see him. Izanagi appears in front with a grin and uses force magic and blasts Akio in his chest, a shock wave powers behind Akio destroying the big building, Akio falls to the ground unconscious.

"What was that move? his magic was so fast it looked like he did not even touch Akio and his magic appeared behind him to destroy the building" Silva thought.

"Okay, everyone on their feet" Izanagi instructs.

Silva stands and walks towards his master, Kaito helps Luna up and they stand beside Silva. Kori still standing still looks at his arm.

"What was that magic I used; it was like someone else was controlling my consciousness" he thought.

He turns and the four stands beside Izanagi waiting on instructions.

"Kaito and Luna, you two free the villagers, Kori and Silva we will round up the dark kingdom members and tie them up, we will take them back to the Kingdom for interrogation" he said.

Everyone plays their part, and the villagers are free, but the village is pretty much destroyed from the battle.

"Do not worry, the Loch Kingdom will pay for damages and rebuild your village" Izanagi tells them.

They thank Izanagi and the others for protecting them against the evil Dark Kingdom.

Kaito

5 – The Others

Behind the Loch Academy is the Loch headquarters, this is where the Grand Loch Warriors meet with the Head Loch Warrior. They have a meeting going on, they discuss how their trainees are doing.

"Izanagi, you fool, why would you let your trainees do a high rank mission, that is dangerous and reckless," said Fumiko Ito.

"Fumi relax, my young Loch Warriors are a very powerful bunch, they protected the villagers and completed the mission, and I could have intervened at any moment as I was watching from a nearby tree," said Izanagi.

"Cocky fool" Fumiko thought.

"She is right, you are responsible for your Loch Warrior's safety, but with all that said tell them Well done from me, but the question in the room is why is the Dark Kingdom attacking small villages," said Ichiro.

"Master Ichiro, the dark kingdom are weak, they attack small villages because that is where we are unlikely going to be as we are assigned to main cities in Loch," said Enji.

"He does have a point, but do not forget the rouge Loch Warrior Rain could be behind the dark Kingdom's resurrection" Izanagi states.

"Rain, his whole thought process on the world is stupid and childish," said Fumiko.

"Didn't you look up to Rain when you was a trainee," said Izanagi.

"I did, but he was also your best friend" she said.

"He was my best friend, us two as a team was unbeatable, but his lust for power drove him down a dark path".

"That is where I take responsibility, I failed to protect his corrupt mind," said Ichiro.

"You did not fail Master, he failed us and when we eventually cross paths, I will end him," said Izanagi.

"Any way on a lighter topic, Xof your son Drake is developing great," said Enji.

"I do not care" said Xof, he sits with his eyes closed and his arms folded.

"Right" said Enji.

Ichiro pulls out six sheets of paper, he places them centre of the table.

"These are missions I need completing, they are information and locations of where the Dark Kingdom may attack next, you may bring your Loch Warrior students, but you will have to accompany them, these missions are extremely dangerous as Rain or Looner Sye may be there" Ichiro explains.

"Yes Master Ichiro" everyone said.

Back at the academy, Kori and Kaito train in the courtyard testing their magical abilities. Luna watches from the benches as she eats an apple.

"Let's give it our all Kaito," said Kori.

"Yeah" said Kaito.

Kori runs at Kaito and goes for a flying kick, his foot misses Kaito's head by an inch as Kaito uses his lightning-fast reflexes to move his head slightly left. Kaito spins and uses Lightening elbow to his Kori in the chest, this sends him flying to the ground. Kori reacts by landing on one hand to use a wooden vine to wrap around the right leg of Kaito.

"His range is crazy" Kaito thought.

He looks down at the vine and covers his hand in lightening to slice the vine off. As he looks up Kori appears before him and knocks him flying with a punch. Kaito looks at Kori's hand and sees he covered his hand with wooden branches.

Kaito stands and smiles, Kori turns as he hears clapping from the right. Suddenly a flash of lightening appears directly in front of Kori and knocks him back, luckily Kori blocked and lands onto his feet.

The lightening vanishes revealing a guy with Black short hair, he smirks at Kori.

"Nice block, I am Jin Tenchi a first year like yourself".

"I see I am Kori Tenkai; I do not appreciate you interrupting mine and Kaito's sparring match".

"You guys were sparring I thought you was playing around like children".

"What did you say? How about I teach you how someone should use lightening magic" said Kaito.

"Kaito Mizuno, I have heard a lot of things about you, but everyone knows the Tenchi family has the superior lightening magic".

"Kori!!".

Kori turns and sees Drake running up to him, he smiles and gives him a thumbs up.

"Drake, long time no see," said Kori.

"Yeah, I see you have met my teammate".

"This jerk is with you?".

"Yeah, in fact we are the strongest team according to Master Ichiro," said Drake.

"What strongest team, maybe the old man has finally lost it" said Kaito.

"Now, now let's not get into my team is better than yours, who cares who the strongest team is" said a girl who stands beside Jin, she has short purple hair with bright orange eyes.

"Who are you?" Kori asked.

"I am Heidi Sye, nice to meet you".

Luna comes over to Kori, "Kori, I think we should go".

"Awe, aren't you cute, what's your name?" Heidi asked.

"Luna Evergrande".

"In fact, we are the strongest, we have one of the strongest first years on our team" said Jin, he points to a guy hiding behind a tree.

"That guy the strongest he's too scare to come from behind the tree" said Kaito.

"He may look fragile and timid, but he is super strong," said Drake.

"Nah, he looks weak" said Kaito.

Kaito looks to the tree and sees that the guy has vanished, suddenly he hears a voice in his hear.

"Who's weak" he said.

Kaito turns and jumps back in defence as the guy's magical energy is immense.

"I'm Junji Kutsuki, I don't like people".

"What a freak?" Kaito thought.

"JUNJI!!!" Kori shouts which startles Junji, "I vow one day I will become the strongest Loch Warrior".

"Erm okay…" Junji muttered.

Jin powers up and goes for an attack on Kori, Kori looks shocked as he is slow at reacting to Jin. As Jin is about to hit Kori, a powerful gust of wind knocks Jin back.

"You losers better watch yourself; I am the strongest," said Silva.

"Wow Silva, where did you come from?" Kori asked.

"I have just arrived, Master Izanagi wants us to meet him out front, now come on".

"Wait, what is your name?" Jin asked.

"Silva Mainz".

"My name is…".

"Did not ask and do not care, let's go guys," said Silva.

Jin is left shocked at Silva's cold shoulder, "Hmm, why does Silva always get the cool moments" Kori thought.

David Drakai watches from a hallway window, staring at Kori and his team walk away.

"David what are you doing?".

"Oh, Seiji I did not see you there".

"I know, you was glaring out of the window".

"Oh, I see, it was nothing, let's go back to the dorms".

"Hello everyone," said Izanagi.

"How come you wanted to see us Izanagi Sensei? is it another mission" Kori asked.

"It is indeed".

"Yes, finally, hopefully I can try a new move I have been working on," said Kori.

"Right, this mission is a very dangerous one, that dangerous I will have to accompany you".

"More dangerous than the last one?" Luna asked.

"Yes, we are to head to a location north, it is said that the leader of the dark kingdom could be at this location".

"The leader of the dark kingdom" Kori thought with rage.

"We set off in two hours, so be ready and meet me at the entrance to the academy".

Looner

6 - Looner

North is the location Team Izanagi head to, there has been report of dark kingdom activity at Port Inquisition a place where ships from other countries trade.

"I wonder who the leader of the Dark Kingdom is?" Kaito wondered.

"A very evil man named Rain, he was once my comrade when I was in the academy" Izanagi explained.

"Wow, you two were once friends, that's crazy, is he strong?" Kori asked.

"Yes, he is strong, obviously not stronger than me, but he isn't too bad at magic use".

"Who cares who he is, I will defeat him," said Silva.

"Yeah, right ha-ha," said Kori.
Everyone walks up the road and up a steep hill, as they reach the top, they see the wide ocean and the port in the distance.

"What a beautiful sight," said Luna.

"Yeah, this is my first time seeing an ocean, that's a lot of water" said Kaito.

"Your first time?" Kori asked.

"Yeah, I grew up in Anthem City, which is located in the middle of Loch so no ocean or seas nearby".

"I see, well it's nothing special, just deep water and big fish really".

"Let's head down to the port everyone," said Izanagi.

Everyone heads into the port; it was very modern as the floor was concrete and the docks were made from metal. The buildings were traditional wood, Izanagi closes his eyes and senses nothing around him.

"It looks like no dark kingdom members are here at the moment, you guys go and talk to the locals find out if any men in cloaks have passed by here, I will speak to the owner of these docks".

"Yes sensei" everyone said.

Izanagi teleports away, this always shocks Kori at how fast his sensei is.

"Right let's split up, because Kori and Kaito are idiots, I will go with Kaito and Luna you go with Kori that way we should get some valuable information," said Silva.

"Yeah, he does have a point, I would have found a place to eat," said Kori.

"You're not meant to agree with him," said Luna.

"Luna let's ask the locals in a bar, then I can eat some food".

"Right, sure".

Silva and Kaito head to the docks to speak to the fishermen while Luna and Kori head to Shark Finns bar to see if anyone knows anything. Kori opens the wooden door and sees a lively bar. People were drinking and playing cards. Kori smiles as this place looks like fun, Luna walks over to the bar and drags Kori along.

"Excuse me bartender, have you seen anyone wearing black cloaks about?" she asked.

"Sorry little miss but I haven't been outside much today".

"Can I order a couple stakes," said Kori.

"Yeah, that will be five gold coins".

"Five, I only have one, Luna do you have any money I can lend".

"Fine, here, but you best eat quick, we need to find some information".

"Black cloaks sounds familiar".

Luna turns and sees an old man sat in the corner.

"Have you seen people in black cloaks?" she asked.

"Yes, come sit I will tell you everything, for two gold coins that is".

"What is it with leaches robbing my money today" she thought.

Luna and Kori sit down at the old man's table, Kori eats his stake like an animal.

"Sorry about him, he wasn't raised correctly," said Luna.

"Ha-ha, that is fine, he reminds me of my son," said the old man.

"So, about the people in black cloaks," said Luna.

"Yes, they arrived early in the morning, they were on a medium sized ship, they were wearing long black cloaks and did not pay the toll to park their ship".

"Yeah, sounds about right, they are a part of the dark kingdom, did you see them pass through or are they still in Port Inquisition?".

"Unfortunately, they passed through about an hour ago, they headed down the west road, but they had a man with them, he did not wear a black cloak he wore a long green jacket with blue pants, his hair was long and spiky and coloured purple, not sure if he was their leader or not but he looked strong".

"Strong, well I will kick his arse and send him back to the ship, do not worry old man," said Kori.

"Old man, please call me Fredrick, I use to be a loch warrior like you when I was young".

"Wow you was a loch warrior, what happened?".

"It was eighteen years ago, I had a son named Atticus, I did not want him to grow up without a father as the missions were getting dangerous each time, they was assigned to me, so I retired and became a ship builder".

"I see understandable, you look happy, and I am sure your son appreciates the sacrifice you did," said Luna.

"He did, he is now a full fledge Loch Warrior himself, I am sure you guys will cross paths with him in the future".

"Atticus, his name sounds familiar," said Kori.

"He was the grand loch warrior who was our proctor in the exam," said Luna.

"Oh yeah, he was super cool".

"I am glad you think so, now you two bests be heading off if you want to catch up to those men," said Frederick.

"You are right, thank you for your time, sir," said Luna.

The mayor lives in a small tower overlooking the docks, Izanagi opens the door and sees the mayor sat looking out from his window he turns his head towards Izanagi.

"You here for news of the dark kingdom?" he asked.

"I am, how did you know?" Izanagi wondered.

"You are Izanagi the strongest Loch warrior, you are famous all over loch, also I know everything about my docks, who leaves and who comes".

"I see, very smart, can you tell me where they went?"

"My fishermen heard them talk about heading west to Cobalt Forest, not sure why as that forest is just full of trees no civilisation anywhere".

"Interesting, maybe they knew we was coming as our source said they would be here around ten minutes ago, maybe in fact we have a traitor, but any way, I think they have a base set up there, thanks for your time, I must head their immediately".

Izanagi teleports out of the room, leaving the mayor confused and angered as he left the door open, Kori and Luna meet up with Silva and Kaito outside the bar, they relay information with each other, which ended up being the same stuff they were told that cloaked men headed down the West Road. Izanagi teleports in front of the team, he looks west and senses magical energy, knowing that the information given was correct.

"I am sure you found out they went west, we must hurry and follow them, another team of Loch Warriors have gone that way as all teams were given missions from sources to pursue, if Looner Sye is with the dark kingdom then that means they are in danger, so come on let's get a move on".

They all run down the muddy road, heading for Cobalt Forest, Kori can also sense huge magic ahead of them, but he smiles at the opportunity to fight someone strong.

"Izanagi sensei, who is Looner Sye? Is he powerful?" Kaito asked.

"He is a scientist for Nortdrum a country north of us, his magic is unheard off and it is unknown why he is with the Dark Kingdom, there are a lot of questions we have, but at this moment we must stop him".

"Understood, which team was sent to this location?".

"Team Enji, they are first years like yourself".

"Oh god, that means we have to deal with that cocky fool," said Kori.

"Yeah, and that creepy girl with the purple hair" said Kaito.

"Purple hair, what was her name?" Izanagi asked.

"It was Heidi Sye," said Luna.

"I see, maybe she is the traitor, she must be related to Looner Sye, he has purple hair, no it is not a must it is a fact" Izanagi thought to himself.

They finally enter Cobalt Forest, they are overwhelmed by its beauty, all the trees had blue leaves, which gives it the name Cobalt.

"A forest of blue leaves, who would have thought this was real" said Kaito.

"Hey Luna, they match your hair," said Kori.

"Oh thanks" she said as she blushes.

Izanagi stops them and instantly looks left, "I sense something left, it is coming towards us fast so be on guard".

The tension builds as the bushes begin to rattle, suddenly Enji, Jin, Drake, Junji and Heidi appear from the bushes.

"Izanagi, what are you doing here?" Enji asked.

"Come to the side I will explain" he said.

Kori and the others look at Jin, they give him dagger stares.

"As if you losers have come all the way here, you know this is an actual mission not some game, right?" said Jin.

"Listen Jim, we came here to assist you as you are not capable of facing a tough opponent," said Kori.

"My name is Jin you spiky haired dweeb".

"Stop acting like children, we are on a mission, we should stand here and wait for our instructions of our sensei's," said Silva.

"Silva Mainz, I heard about you, Mr Wind magic, well news flash my magic is so much more powerful than yours," said Jin.

"Who cares if his magic sucks, he is still cute," said Heidi.

"Ugh, why does Silva get a compliment of a girl while I am stood right next to him" Kaito thought.

Izanagi and Enji gather the teams together for an announcement, "listen up everyone, from this point forward we will be working together on this mission, we will head to a base just up ahead that is where the dark kingdom are, we are to find out what is going on, they have a dangerous magic user with them so we must tread carefully" Izanagi explained.

"Did Izanagi sensei not say Looner Sye so he could get Heidi's reaction when she sees him in person, after all she maybe a spy" Kori thought.

They all travel further into the forest until the path disappears, Enji spots a white building just through the trees.

"That is where they went, I can sense magical energy in that direction".

"Good work Master your magic sense is next to none," said Drake.

"Why thank you young Drake," said Enji.

"Suck up" Kaito thought.

They head to a steep hill that is pretty high up, so they are able to watch over the building, Enji watches through a small telescope.

"I see five men in cloaks, they seem to be patrolling the area of the building".

"I see, Kori, Jin and Heidi, you three will come with me, we will sneak to the left wing of the building and try and find a way into their," said Izanagi.

They all slide down the steep hill while Drake, Silva, Kaito and Luna watch, Silva was given instructions from Izanagi that if anyone else appears he is to use his wind magic to create a small and cold breeze so that Izanagi knows.

Kori and the others force their way through the steel fence and head straight for the corner of the building. Kori peaks around and sees the five men walk in the opposite direction.

"Izanagi sensei they are walking the other way, shall I take them out?" Kori asked.

"No, we cannot attract attention, let's find a way in and gather as much information as possible".

"Look, there is a vent above one of the doors over there, if we can get in then surly we can eve's drop on them" said Jin.

"Correct, very good Jin, let's go everyone," said Izanagi.

Heide uses her magic to pull of the metal vent door, she uses this from psychic magic as it levitates off and slowly comes to the ground.

"Wow that was so cool," said Kori.

Izanagi heads into the vent first followed by the others, they crawl to a point where they are on top of another vent door, Izanagi looks through and can see into the huge room. He sees men in long white coats stood around a huge cylinder with boiling green stuff inside.

"Right, everyone, be as quiet as you can, I am going to listen in to see what they are planning" Izanagi instructed.

Below in the building, Looner Sye walks up to his men, he places his hand on the cylinder.

"Everything looks to be going as planned, Master will not be disappointed with this, now let's speak about the transfer" he stated.

"Yes Looner, Master will need a capsule's worth of M-D118, his body will be able to handle that amount".

"Thanks Doctor Hennessey, sort that out for me and I will be on my way" said Looner.

He gets his men to pull out a small golden capsule, they wear thick black gloves as they fill it up.

"M-D118, what the hell is that?" Izanagi questioned to himself.

Looner stops and smirks, his eyes gaze up, "so we have intruders do we" he thought.

Looner raises his hand and uses psychic magic to bring the whole vent system down to the ground. Izanagi lands on his feet while the others land roughly.

"Spiky blonde hair, Izanagi Suzuki, what a great honour to meet you" said Looner.

"Likewise, the crazy scientist of the Dark Kingdom, Looner Sye," said Izanagi.

Looner looked shocked as he spots Heidi stand up with the others.

"I see, an offspring of mine".

"Sye, how do you have the same last name as me?" Heidi asked.

"Well, I am your father, I see your filthy mother did not even mention me to you, what a shame, I would have liked to have someone with powers like mine with the Dark Kingdom".

"So, Heidi is not the traitor, she did not even know Looner was her father, then who could it be" Izanagi thought.

"Hey, do not disrespect her mother, it was you who was absent from her life, so why would she want to know that her father is a creepy criminal!!" Kori shouted.

"Insolent boy, you should know your place" said Looner.

Looner pushes his hand forward and knocks Kori flying into a container using his psychic magic. Izanagi springs into action and goes for an impact punch, but he stands frozen as his fist was about to hit Looner.

"The thing with my magic is I can use any part of my body to control things, the real secret is my bright orange eyes" Looner explained.

"Sorry but my magic does not need to touch you, as long as you are in my radius you do not stand a chance".

Izanagi releases his impact magic and destroys the cylinder and launching Looner through a wall along with his minions.

"Damn, Izanagi sensei's magic is insane..." Jin muttered.

Heidi helps Kori to his feet, he thanks her and looks to Izanagi, he smiles but Izanagi begins to fall to the floor.

"Izanagi sensei!!" Kori shouted.

Looner appears in front of Izanagi and uses hypnosis magic to render Izanagi unconscious.

"Your strength did not disappoint, but we have studied you for the past few years, now I know I cannot beat you so I must send you away while I kill your young Loch Warriors".

Looner uses his magic to levitate Izanagi and sends him through the roof and far away from the building site.

"Bastard, I will not let you get away with this," said Kori.

Looner teleports in front of Kori, and Kori is shocked by his magical energy, it was immense.

"I have to use it" Kori quickly thought.

Kori quickly slaps the ground hard, "Grand Tree!!" he yells.

A huge tree shoots from the ground destroying the roof and most of the building. A huge smoke cloud is created as everyone was shocked, Kori stands breathing heavily hoping his attack has destroyed Looner Sye.

Enji

7 – Looner vs Enji

Enji and the others watch from the cliff, they see the tree tower from within the building.

"That tree must be over one hundred metres tall, where did it come from?" Enji wondered.

"That is wood magic, Kori's magic, something must have happened, we need to get down there and assist," said Silva.

"Let's go, be on alert, do not do something you cannot handle, if I say we retreat we retreat" Enji instructed.

Inside the building, Heidi and Jin get up from the ground, the tree took up all the room in the building.

"Next time you do that can you give us a bit more warning," said Jin.

"Sorry, I felt his killing intent, I had no choice but to unleash my full power attack," said Kori.

"Not a bad attack, that is like a level of a grade two Loch Warrior, you have potential".

Kori looks to the tree route and sees Looner standing there, not a scratch on him.

"Damn, he dodged my attack".

"My magic is Psychic, but I have two infinities I can also use gravity magic" Looner explained.

He points three of his fingers towards Kori, Jin, and Heidi, he uses gravity force, they all fall to the ground and are unable to move.

Kaito dashes through the wall and uses Lightening strike to knock Looner back, freeing Kori and the others from his gravity magic.

"Nice one Kaito," said Kori.

"Anytime" said Kaito.

Silva, Luna, and Enji appear at the side of Kori and the others.

"Sorry we took so long, it's like the building suppresses magic, as soon as that tree spawned, we was able to sense magical energy being used," said Enji.

"Where is Izanagi Sensei?" Luna asked.

"That bastard used a weird move to put him to sleep then he used his psychic magic to send him flying from here" Kori explained.

"Wait, how come we did not detect that?" Silva wondered.

"I had an instinct that there were others so I cloaked his energy with my own which cannot be detected, but that is fine, I can take you all easy" said Looner.

"Let's not get ahead of ourselves Looner, I will be the one to stop you, after all I am a Grand Loch Warrior," said Enji.

Looner teleports in front of Enji and uses his hands to levitate Enji, he raises him in the air.

"Enji sensei!!" Heidi shouts.

Enji focuses all his magical energy into his legs and shoots heat directly at Looner causing the ground to explode. Enji knows it is not over and uses heatwave to move the smoke away and to heat up what was in front of him. Looner kneeling down uses a force field around him so he can be protected from the heat.

"Smart, usually people melt when I release this attack," said Enji.

"So, he is Enji the heat magic user, impressive, this may be harder than I thought" Looner thought.

Looner looks at Jin and pulls him towards him by levitating him closer and in front of the heat attack. Enji sees this and stops his heat magic; he clenches his fist with anger.

"You coward!!" Enji shouted.
Jin turns and thunder stomps, breaking Looner's lock on him. Silva quickly sends a wind beam at Looner, he deflects it by using his psychic magic, flinging it to the right wall.

"Damn how can we beat this guy?" Kori wondered.

Enji teleports behind Looner and elbows him in the back, Looner is surprised by his speed. Looner turns and swings his leg to use a roundhouse kick, Enji blocks this with his right arm and quickly uses his left hand to heat blast Looner through the huge tree.

"Wow, Enji Sensei is super strong" Kori thought.

Looner brushes of the dust from his shoulders, he looks angered.

"This may be more troublesome than I thought... what to do..." he muttered.

Enji takes up a martial arts stance as his arms begin to glow with steam radiating from his veins.

"Damn, I guess this is the power of a grand loch warrior, it's just my luck that two came together, I need to deliver this veil to the master" Looner thought.

"Turn yourself in and I will show you mercy," said Enji.

Looner smirks, he stands back up and begins to look around. Enji sees he is looking to escape so he rushes Looner and begins a barrage of heat infused palm attacks. Looner struggles to dodge as a few connect with his body. Looner quickly uses repel and knocks Enji back a few yards. Enji slams the ground and blasts Looner below with a huge heat blast. Looner flies in the air, hurt from the devastating attack.

"Have the same fate as Izanagi" said Looner.

He looks into the eyes of Enji and uses hypnosis magic, Enji smiles, "why are you smiling, my magic should be working" said Looner.

"Your hypnosis will not work on me Looner, I have covered my entire body is heat magic, this will burn any magic you throw at me".

"You bastard" said Looner, he begins to sweat as he lands back onto his feet.

"Speaking of Izanagi" said Enji as he looks to his left.

Something crashes down and causes the ground to shake, the dust clears, and Izanagi has returned, his face was full of rage as he glared at Looner Sye.

"Just because you tricked me once, does not mean you will trick me again, you creepy freak," said Izanagi.

"Izanagi sensei" Kori said with joy.

Looner looked worried, he was out of options to escape, a voice communicates in the back of Looner's mind.

"Looner, do you have the veil?".

"Master Rain is that you?" Looner asked within his mind.

"It is, I see you are in a bit of a pickle".

"I am, there are two grand Loch Warriors and eight loch warriors, I don't know if I will be able to escape".

"Nonsense, I have sent Normir".

"Normir the plague, one of the five divine generals of the dark kingdom, so you knew I would be ambushed".

"It is only natural that we have a backup plan, now on the signal, escape and return to me".

Izanagi powers up and is ready to release an impact punch. Orange mist begins to enter the room, Izanagi stops and sees this.

"Orange mist, what is this?".

Izanagi looks up and sees a pale man dressed in a black cloak sending orange mist from his hands. Looner spots Normir and uses his magic to pull the rest of the roof down upon Izanagi and the others. Izanagi uses impact punch and destroys all the debris from the roof. He looks over to Looner and sees he has vanished. The orange mist begins to smell like gas, Enji notices this and nods to Heidi to use her magic. Heidi levitates everyone and they fly away from the lab.

"Why are we flying away?" Kori asked.

The lab explodes into a huge blast, Kori looked shocked, "that was a close call" he said.

They land safely on top of the cliff from where they started. Izanagi does not look happy as he looks towards the explosion.

"Izanagi, surely we can catch them if we set off now," said Enji.

"It's no use, they are high level magic users, they have covered their magical energy so that it would be impossible to sense, lets head back to the academy and inform Ichiro," said Izanagi.

"Hey punk," said Jin.

"You talking to me," said Silva.

"Yeah, just because we did a mission together does not mean we are friends, I will become the most powerful".

"If you wish, but that is impossible as I will become the strongest," said Silva.

"You two idiots, I am the one to become the strongest Loch Warrior," said Kori.

"Man, boys are such idiots," said Heidi.

"Yeah" said Luna.

Izanagi.

8 - Brume Tower

A few weeks have passed by since the encounter with Looner. Kori and his team have been on many low rank missions and have succeeded in all of them. But Kori was not happy with the low rank missions, he wanted a dangerous one.

Izanagi, Kori, Kaito, Silva and Luna are inside Ichiro's office, he sits in a chair behind a small wooden desk.

"Welcome Team Izanagi, I am very impressed with the work you have been doing," said Ichiro.

"Thank you" said Luna and Kaito.

"Hey old geezer, enough with these kid missions, when are we going to get a proper mission?" said Kori.

"Kori, you can't speak to Master Ichiro like that," said Luna.

"It's alright, I understand how you feel, you feel like you are being underused," said Ichiro.

"Yeah, like I want a mission where we can finally take down the dark kingdom".

"You are not ready for that type of mission young man, at your level now, you would be destroyed by a general of the dark kingdom".

Kori looked confused, "these missions are for you to become experienced and work together as a team and what it truly means to be a Loch Warrior".

"Ichiro, how come you called us here, was it to just give us praise?" Izanagi asked.

"Well as young Kori wanted a hard mission, I have an important mission for your team, Brume Tower located north has been taken over by a dark magic user, as I have a separate mission for you Izanagi, I want your team to report to Fumiko".

"Thank you, old man, I am so excited to show you I can handle a hard mission" Kori excitingly said.

"Master Ichiro, who is Fumiko?" Kaito asked.

"She is a grand loch warrior, you four will accompany her and a few members of her team to Brume tower and take down this dark magic user".

"Understood master, let's go guys," said Silva.

"Good luck all of you, do not do something stupid and listen to what instructions Fumiko has," said Izanagi.

They leave the room and head to find Fumiko, Izanagi closes the door and turns to Ichiro.

"What mission will I be going on?" Izanagi asked.

"I need you to head to Nortdrum, find out where the base of the dark kingdom is and report back, a war is brewing between the two countries".

"I see, very well then, I will see you soon old man".

Fumiko waits down a hallway for Kori and the others, Kori looks ahead and sees a woman.

"Are you Fumiko sensei?" Kori asked.

"Yes, I am" she said, "oh my god he called me sensei I love it" she thought.

"Right, I have seen your images so no need for introductions, brown spiky hair is Silva Mainz, blondie is Kaito Mizuno, kid with black hair and blue jacket is Kori Tenkai and blue hair is Luna Evergrande, nice to meet you all, I am Fumiko Ito".

"Nice to meet you, Fumiko sensei, we are very excited to go on a high rank mission" said Kaito.

"I see, well I will be bringing two of my second years along with us, hopefully they can teach you all a thing or two," said Fumiko.

Two members of team Fumiko walk around the corner to greet the first years, one was a beautiful girl with medium length orange hair with green leaf clips on the right side of her head, she had green eyes and wore a brown leather jacket with beige pants. She introduced herself as Aithne Agni, the other was David Drakai.

"Wait that tall man is not a second year I saw him in the examinations," said Kori.

"True, but he is from another country, he was a part of the Asros knights, so considering he is sixteen years old he was moved to the second years, he only did the exam so he could get use to how we operate" Fumiko explained.

David glares at Kori, "why does he always give me an evil death stare" Kori thought.

"Right, everyone, let me explain the mission, we are heading to Brume Tower, this place is located north, a tower built on the cliff of an active volcano, a dark magic user who is currently unnamed has taken the tower hostage, intel say he is going to mine into the volcano and cause it to erupt, we are to take him out and bring him into custody".

"Yes Sensei" everyone said.

They travel north in horse and carriage; it takes them around ten hours to reach the outskirts of the volcano. Kori looks out the carriage and sees the huge tower on the side of the volcano. The tower was tall with obsidian bricked walls, black smoke radiated from the top of the tower as it was originally used for mining coal and other materials.

"Kaito look, it is huge," said Kori.

"It is, but that volcano looks scary" said Kaito.

"Don't be alarmed because the volcano has not erupted for over two hundred years" Silva explained.

"That is not very assuring" said Kaito.
The carriage stops and everyone exits it, Fumiko pats the horse and tells it to go ten minutes south.

"We will walk on foot from here, remember we cannot be spotted so be stealthy" she instructed.

"Can't really be stealthy with this six-foot eight monster with us," said Kori.

"Well, we all can't be blessed with being an absolute dwarf like you," said David.

"Hey, I will have you know I am very close to average height".

"Guys come on let's head out," said Aithne.

Fumiko and the team scale the left side of the volcano to find the path that leads towards Brume Tower. Silva stops as he feels uneasy, he begins to sweat and look a bit nervous.

"What's wrong Silva?" Luna asked.

"I sense intense dark magical energy from the top of the tower".

"Impressive, a young loch warrior like him being able to sense magical energy from this distance" Fumiko thought.

"Does not matter how strong his magical energy is, I will beat his face in," said Kori.

"Yeah" Kaito agreed.

"Fools" David thought.

They reach the black gates of Brume Tower; they crouch behind a few boulders as they see men patrolling the bottom of the tower.

"Kori and David, you two distract the guards walking the bottom, once distracted the rest of us will enter the tower," said Fumiko.

Kori and David sneak over to the tower, three men wearing torn leather armour walk towards them wielding short swords.

"You got any tricks little man?" David asked.

"I do, watch this".

Kori places his hand on the ground, he focuses and behind the men, he uses wood magic to create small and silent vines to shoot from the ground behind them. The vines wrap around the legs of the right man and trips him.

"Hey, watch where you are walking, we are guards".

"Sorry, I did not see a vine in front of me".

"Wait a vine, why is a vine on a volcano surely the heat would incinerate it".

"Dave, you turn," said Kori.

"My name is David".

David uses ice magic and places his hand on the floor freezing the three men and the floor in the process.

"Wow, ice magic is so cool" Kori said.

Fumiko and the others reach the entrance and walk inside. Kori and David go to the door, but it slams shut. Kori uses the handle, and it will not open.

"What the hell?" Kori thought.

David uses his ice magic to freeze the door, he then swings a hard punch at the door, but the ice cracks off at the power of the punch but the door still would not open.

"Guy's the door won't open, it is bound by a magical seal, we have to defeat the caster for it to open, you will have to wait there," said Fumiko.

"Awe man, I wanted a piece of the action" Kori moaned.

Fumiko and the others head to the first floor, the stairs are blocked by a magical seal. Next to Fumiko was a door, she opens it, and they walk into a huge wide room.

"So, we can go for the door but cannot go upstairs" she said.

"Maybe there are levels to this, kinda like a game," said Silva.

"Guys look ahead," said Aithne.

A skinny man with short blonde hair and red baggy pants on stands up from sitting down.

"Welcome challengers, if you want to advance you will have to beat me, if you successfully beat me you can go to the second floor for the next challenge if you beat all challenges and get to the top you will be able to face the master, my name is Asahi".

"Fumiko sensei, let me take this one," said Silva.

"Sure thing, there are five floors so after this Aithne fights, I will fight the master," said Fumiko.

"Aithne..., Fumiko sensei truly believes she is strong, but how strong could she be" Silva thought.

"Good luck Silva," said Luna.

"Yeah, make sure you don't lose or me and Kori will make fun of you" said Kaito.

Silva smirks, "do not worry I got this".

Silva steps forward, he powers up his magical energy while looking at Asahi with a serious facial expression. Asahi smiles and begins to power up also, Silva senses his magical energy and is happy that this guy is powerful. Silva uses wind magic and sends a thick gust of wind at Asahi, knocking him a few feet back. Asahi teleports in front of Silva and elbows him in the face, Silva in pain almost lands on his back but spins and kicks Asahi in the ribs.

"Ugh!!" Asahi grips his side in pain, Silva uses wind magic to lift Asahi of the ground. Asahi uses Mercury magic to create a scythe, he swings hard and stops the wind from lifting him up by slicing it in half.

"A metal type magic, mercury, this may be troublesome" Silva thought.

"Damn, he cut through Silva's magic with one swing" said Kaito.

"Silva..." Luna muttered.

Asahi quickly attacks Silva, swinging hard forcing Silva to use his reflexes to dodge each attack, but Silva can feel the force behind the swings. Asahi launches the scythe at the floor right in front of Silva, the scythe quickly turns into a mercury puddle and latches onto Silva's boots.

"Crap I can't move," said Silva.

Asahi covered his hand in mercury, this made his fist shiny and silver.

"My fist is as strong as steel, are you ready to perish young man," said Asahi.

Asahi sprints forward, his fist was clenched tight, and he draws it back ready for a hard punch. Silva worried uses a strong attack to knock Asahi back, a small tornado, it swirls him around and knocks him into the left wall. Silva uses wind slash to tear his boots enough so he can take them off.

"You are a smart one boy," said Asahi.

"I have had enough!!, I will end this now," said Silva.

Asahi covers his whole body in mercury, "try your best attack, you cannot break my mercury defences".

"Just watch me".

Silva screams as he puts his palms close together, a wind ball begins to form between his hands, the wind is that fast it becomes visible. Asahi begins to run towards Silva, he turns his right hand into a sword and goes for a swing, Silva ready launches the ball at Asahi, the ball hits his stomach at an incredible speed and begins to crack the mercury. The ball explodes and shoots Asahi through the brick wall and far away from Brume tower, he becomes a dot in the distance.

"Yeah, go on Silva" said Kaito.

"Very good kid, your power is almost on par with a grade 2 loch warrior" Fumiko thought.

Fumiko

9 – Level two

Silva is victorious which means the barrier has now vanished. Fumiko and the others make their way up the stairs onto the second floor of the tower. She opens the door and sees that the whole room is covered in grass and trees.

"How is this possible?" Luna asked.

"Could this be an illusion or is this the effects of someone's magic?" Silva wondered.

"This is the effect of my magic".

Everyone looks around to see who said that, from behind a tree a man with purple hair tied into a bun walks around, his eyes were yellow, and he wore a white gown.

"I see you defeated Asahi, I am impressed, but if you think you stand a chance against me then you are hugely mistaken".

"Who are you?" Fumiko asked.

"My name is Lillic".

Aithne steps up with a huge smile, her right fist is cased in fire as she punches the palm of her other hand.

"Lillic I am your challenger; I am Aithne Agni, and I will defeat you".

"Her magical energy is insane, is she really only a year above us" Silva thought.

"Fire magic, how cute, I hope you're ready to die girl".

Aithne uses speed magic to teleport behind Lillic and smashes him with a fire fist causing an explosion, smoke covers the room.

The smoke begins to clear and Lillic stands unhurt by the attack, his face looked disappointed.

"What?" Aithne was stunned.

"Weak…" Lillic said.

A red flower blooms on the tree right of Aithne, it had a mouth that smirked. Aithne sees this and looks nervous; the flower shoots a small white lighted beam through her arm. Blood drips down her arm from the small hole formed from the light beam, Aithne destroys the flower with a fire fist punch.

"As you see that was just one of many flowers I have created, I have the power to create natural resources" said Lillic.

"You have power that can help people and you waste it being a criminal," said Aithne.

"Why would I help disgusting peasants, I will be rich and rule Loch with my master".

Aithne appears in front of Lillic and punches him in the gut, she releases a barrage of punches on Lillic and ends it with a flame kick, knocking Lillic through three trees.

"She is so powerful," said Luna.

"She is one of the strongest second years and the second strongest on my team," said Fumiko.

"Second strongest?" Silva asked.

"David is the strongest on my team, his ice magic is powerful".

Lillic sits up, he wipes the blood from his lip, he looks at Aithne with frustration wondering how she is so fast.

Lillic stands and raises his arms to summon twenty flowers, Aithne closes her eyes and enters a calm state. The flowers shoot multiple beams towards her, the beams travel faster than the eye can see but Aithne with her eyes closed, dodges each beam attack. Silva reacts with shock as he knows she has magic sense which allows her to sense magic through her body.

Lillic looked scared as he stands back up, his hair falls down as his hair band snaps.

"Admit defeat," said Aithne.

Lillic's yellow eyes begin to glow, the grass and pants begin to attach to his body. Black veins begin to show over his face and the whiteness in his eyes turn black.

"This is full divine transformation".
Lillic has become one with his plants, his arms were pulsating as they were covered in vines. He had two huge red flowers on his shoulders, Aithne tries to concentrate her magical energy as she feels his energy beginning to rise. Lillic shoots a beam at Aithne she dodges but Lillic appears next to her left shoulder, he smashes her to the ground with his fists and kicks her up to the roof. She begins to fall as Lillic shoots two huge beams at her, she covers herself with flames to limit the damage from the beams.

Silva and Kaito step forward they feel they need to help but Fumiko stops them.

"This is her battle; do not underestimate her she will find a way to win," said Fumiko.

Aithne lands on her feet, but she is damaged, she has cuts over her body. Lillic is not done he rushes Aithne and attacks with hand-to-hand combat, Aithne does a good job at blocking and unleashes a lot of fire fists. Lillic tanks the punches and smashes Aithne in the gut causing her to vomit blood. The flowers on his shoulders begin to charge another beam attack. Aithne jumps back and uses fire breath to cover Lillic with flames. The beams shoot through the fire, Aithne jumps and spins dodging the attacks. Lillic looks frustrated as his chest opens revealing a black flower.

"That flower is bigger than the others, I must take it out before it can attack" Aithne thought.

The black flower begins to absorb the life out of the trees and grass in its surroundings. A huge ball of light forms in front of its mouth, it was getting ready to launch a massive beam. Aithne concentrates her magic; steam radiates from her body. Aithne covers her fist in fire and enhances this by making her fist even larger. She uses fire explosion on the bottom of her feet to launch herself at Lillic, she moves fast making Lillic sweat as his attack is almost done.

"Come on hurry up" Lillic begins to panic.

She uses her fire fist to smash the ball of light into the mouth of the black flower knocking him to the back wall causing a massive explosion that makes the whole tower shake.

Aithne falls to the ground exhausted; Fumiko and the others rush over to see if she is okay. The smoke clears and Lillic is back into his normal form unconscious below the massive hole in the wall.

"Did I win?" Aithne asked.

"You did, good job Athine," said Fumiko.

Fumiko helps Aithne stand, her injuries were quite bad, Luna comes over and begins to use soul healing magic.

"You can heal?" Aithne asked.

"Not very well but I can heal the holes the beams made the cuts will have to go on their own as my magical energy is not as great as everyone else's" Luna said.

"Hey, I did not know your soul magic can do that, very nice Luna" said Kaito.

Outside the tower, Kori begins kicking rocks at the side of the volcano in frustration.

"Kicking rocks will not get us inside," said David.

"I know but I can sense everyone's magical energy, they must be having so much fun," said Kori.

"Hey, come over here" said David, he gestures Kori to come towards him.

"What is it, Dave?".

"My name is David you short arse, use your wood magic to create a staircase to the top of this tower".

"Oh yeah I can use wood magic, very smart idea, right let's so this".

Kori places his hands on the floor and focuses his magical energy, wood begins to shoot from the ground, it was in the shape of stairs as he almost reaches the top window of the tower. The wood begins to shake, Kori looks up in confusion. A blue veil begins to surround the tower and absorbs the stairs.

"What the hell, is this the magical barrier that is stopping us going inside?" Kori asked.

"It seems our magic is useless against this barrier" David said as he charges up his magical energy.

David shoots ice shards at the door but the barrier does not budge. Kori joins in by using wood fist to cover his fist in hard wood as he punches the barrier.

From the top window, a man whose face is covered by the shadows looks down at Kori and David as they try everything to break in, the man smirks and walks away from the window.

Athine Agni

10 – Soul Witch

They all head to the third floor, Fumiko is first to open the door, the room was not very bright as someone appears from the shadows from the back of the room. It appears to be a woman with long black hair and wearing a purple robe.

"I am Kano, master has told me he is not happy that you are already on the third level, so he sent me to stop you from going any further".

Kaito steps forward smiling at the chance of fighting.

"Kaito, let me fight this one, save yourself for the next floor," said Luna.

"Yeah okay, do not lose Luna, you got this" Kaito said as he tries to encourage Luna.

"You are a frigid girl, this should be easy work," said Kano.

Luna walks forward, she sends a jellyfish bomb at Kano, the jellyfish lit up the room with his light blue aura, it flew at Kano and explodes.

Luna still senses Kano inside the smoke, knowing that Luna quickly went defensive. The smoke clears and a huge green ball surrounded Kano, it vanishes, and Kano is perfectly fine not even a scratch.

"That was some power, I see you are a witch from the east island," said Kano.

"How do you know that?" Luna confusingly asked.

"Because I am from that area, I am a banished witch, that is when I found my master and joined up to do better for the world".

"Well, I am not like you, I left on my own to become a great loch warrior".

Luna releases another Jellyfish bomb from her finger, Kano summons a black wood staff and uses this to direct the Jellyfish to the left wall destroying it. Luna is shocked that Kano has summoned a witch's staff.

"Seeing your energy and your attacks it would seem you only know one technique," said Kano.

Luna looked serious at those comments, she knew that what she was saying was right, "can I even win" she thought.

Ten years ago in Shroud Village, the witch association is planning on announcing the next line of witches for the celebration. Six-year-old Luna watches from her window as all the young witches line up in front of a small crowd. Luna's mother a woman with long blue hair is the leader of the witches and is stood in front of the young witches.

"Good morning, everyone, today we celebrate these young witches as they become full fledge witches of the Loch Kingdom" said Luna's mother.

"Miss Evergrande, the king is here to see you," said Marius.

"I see, well then, ladies and gentlemen, be back here for sun fall, we will cast the spell of Olette and begin the celebration".

Everyone cheers as Marius looks over to Luna watching from the window, Luna ducks down and crawls to her bed.

"My mother is always busy; I wish she would cast spells with me" Luna thought as she turns and hugs her pillow.

Inside the Witches council room sits King Tulkar the first, he has short blonde hair with a thick beard, his armour was golden as he looks at Evelyn Evergrande walk through the door with his light blue eyes.

"Your majesty, what is the occasion?" Evelyn asked.

"Evelyn, it is always a pleasure to see you, I came to see your witch's celebration, after all I am the king of Loch".

"Well, you are in for a treat, we have eight witches for tonight's celebration the most we have ever had in recent years".

Later that night the witches would perform a ritual that was watched by the whole village. The king sat next to my mother as they enjoyed watching the young witches use their magic. I watched with the other younglings and then my life would get turned upside down.

A portal opened and a woman with long black hair and yellow dragon like eyes stepped from the portal.

Evelyn stands up, her face looked like she seen a ghost as she began to tremble with fear.

"Is this part of the ritual?" King Tulkar asked.

"No, that is Aldia the black dragon of death, she is the most powerful witch in existence" Evelyn explained.

Aldia looks up to Evelyn and smirks as Aldia raises her arm in the air. Everyone looked confused as they gaze up to the sky and see the dark night being lit up by something past the clouds.

"Damn, everyone run away!!" Evelyn shouted.

Luna and the other younglings run for shelter, Evelyn summons her staff into her right hand, smashing through the clouds a huge fire ball comes crashing down upon the village destroying everything in its process. The smoke clears and everyone has been protected by a huge green dome. Luna looks over to her mother and sees that she used a defence spell to protect everyone from the fire ball.

"Impressive Evelyn, but you do know I can do that spell multiple times right," said Aldia.

Evelyn falls to her knees; her magical energy is running low.

"Marius ready the knights, we need to stop this monster" King Tulkar instructed.

Aldia raises her hand once again; Evelyn grips her fists and bows her head to Aldia.

"I beg you, please do not harm anyone here, they are all my family," said Evelyn.

"Ha, family, do not make me sick, you witches are the reason he is sealed, once I find that grimoire, I shall release him".

Luna runs as fast as she can and stands in front of her mother with her arms out.

"If you want to hurt my mother then you have to get past me," said Luna.

"A little girl that doesn't have great magical energy, how pathetic".

"Luna, stop and run away, please," said Evelyn.

"Well try and stop five huge fire balls little girl," said Aldia.

"No, I will not let you hurt my mother and friends".

Luna's magical energy becomes heavy and flows out of her body, the magical energy is visible and is blue with white tints on it, the energy formed above Luna. A jellyfish began to take form, a jellyfish bigger than the original fire ball from Aldia. Luna screams and sends the jellyfish at Aldia; she does block but the power is so great it begins pushing her back. Evelyn quickly opens a portal behind Aldia and the jellyfish explodes sending Aldia through the portal in which Evelyn closes.

After that day the witches would relocate the village so Aldia would not find them in the future, Luna does not remember how she got full control of her energy so that is why she went to Loch Academy to master her skills.

"I will not lose, so what if I only know one attack, if I can make that attack more powerful than anything you have, I will win," said Luna.

Kano does not look happy; she points her staff at Luna and shoot a green beam directly at her. Luna tanks the hit by blocking with her hands, Luna focuses and controls her magical energy by creating a focus point above her head. The floor vibrates as the magical energy forms into a massive blue and white jellyfish above Luna's head.

"That might be the most powerful Jellyfish I have ever seen Luna summon," said Silva.

Luna is finished and raises her hands above her head, she begins to absorb the jellyfish into her hands, making her hands glow white with blue outlines appearing around her hand.

"What is she doing?" Kano thought.

"I have to be stronger, Silva, Kori and Kaito always train to better themselves, I will not be left behind" Luna thought to herself.

Luna closes her hands and places them in a fighting stance, she pushes her first fist forward and a blue orb shoot from her fist and smashes into Kano's chest, knocking her against the wall. Luna sees this as an opening and throws multiple air punches sending multiple orbs at Kano, the orbs keep coming as they explode on impact with Kano.

"Amazing" said Fumiko.

Kano falls to the floor; Luna turns quoting she is victorious. Kano looks up with sadness at her defeat.

"How could I lose to such a weakling; master is going to kill me" Kano thought.

The barrier opens, Kaito steps forward first and turns to everyone.

"Now it is my turn, I shall get a quick victory so we can reach the top" said Kaito.

11 – Lightening vs Sound

Outside Kori and David are tired from all the attacks they have used on the magical barrier on the main door.

"I may have one more trick," said Kori.

David listens as Kori walks up to the door and places his hand on the barrier.

"Creepy voice in my head, if you can hear me, lend me your power to destroy this barrier" Kori thought.

"No, get lost, do you think I care about you helping your friends, I hope they all die horrible deaths," said the voice.

"What the hell voice, stop being so stubborn and help".

"Alright, how about we make a deal, I am sure there is something you want" Kori asked.

"Interesting, let's make a pact, I will help you now but later down the line you will help me".

"Okay voice let's do this".

Kori's eyes glow red, a magical energy flows out of him, and the barrier reacts to it but is overpowered by the intense feeling. Kori punches the barrier, and it shatters as the door is now available to open.

"What was that power?" David questioned.

"Oh, it's nothing, I have a voice in my head that lends me magical energy".

"Right, because that makes sense".

Kori opens the door, David smiles as they both enter Brume Tower.

On the fourth floor, Kaito and the others open the door, Kaito walks into the room and sees a man meditating at the back.

"You there, I am your challenger, I am Kaito Mizuno".

The man stands, he is topless and wears baggy white pants, his hair was pink and tied into a knot. He turns and gazes his silver-coloured eyes at Kaito.

"Nice to meet you Kaito, I am Oto, let's get started, I am very surprised you all managed to beat everyone below me, but this is the furthest you will get, I am the sound god and the right hand man of the master".

"Sound god" Kaito thought.

Kaito powers up his magical energy and zap dashes at Oto, Kaito goes for a lightening punch as he punches his fist passes through Oto. He is shocked as Oto hammer fists Kaito in the back knocking him into the ground. Oto goes for a stomp, Kaito quickly spins dodging his stomp by an inch. Oto's foot hits the ground and sends a sound wave hurting peoples hears. Kaito covers his ears as the sound is loud and unbearable.

Oto moves as fast as sound to kick Kaito into the air, he kicks Kaito ten times within a second and sends Kaito flying into a wall.

"I will not lie kid; I am very disappointed with your performance," said Oto.

Kaito lies against the wall, blood drips from his nose and mouth.

"Kaito, do not give up" Luna shouted.

Kaito looks over to his friends, they are rooting for him to get back up. Kaito slaps himself in his face and stands back up.

"What am I doing, I told them I will win quick so that is what I will do" Kaito thought.

Kaito charges his energy, yellow lightening surged from his whole body, he moves at lightning speed and appears behind Oto and thunder claps him the back knocking him forward, Oto teleport and they both exchange in hand-to-hand combat that could not be seen by the eye.

"So fast, I cannot see them strike each other" said Silva.

Kaito's inexperience begins to show as Oto is faster and more gifted in hand-to-hand combat, he strikes Kaito in the face with a sound breaker fist. Kaito falls slowly to the ground, Oto teleports back to where he started, he laughs as Kaito smashes into the floor.

"Kaito Mizuno, you are a true warrior, one day you could be my equal, but because of situations I will have to kill you".

Oto points his finger at Kaito and sends a sound cutter directly at him, the others are not fast enough to react, and they stand frozen. An ice shard shatters in front of Kaito. Oto looks towards the door and sees David and Kori stood glaring at Oto.

"Kori, David how did you get past the barrier?" Fumiko asked.

"It's a long story, I used a magic that I am not familiar with, but enough of that, who is this guy and why is Kaito on the floor" Kori was raged.

"The master did not anticipate you two to get through the barrier, but no matter who is my next challenger".

"It's m…" Kori said but was interrupted by Fumiko.

"I will be your next challenger," said Fumiko.

"But Sensei I have been outside punching a barrier for a long time, I really want to beat this guy up," said Kori.

"No, he is too dangerous, I am not sure what there master is like, but he cannot be as fast as Oto is, so for now, Luna take Kaito and wait at the bottom of the tower, Kori' David, Silva, and Aithne head to the top of the tower and take out the master of these clowns, Kori can break the barrier".

"Yes Sensei" everyone said.

Luna puts Kaito on her back and wishes everyone good luck as she heads down the spiralling stairs. Fumiko steps forward and releases her immense magical energy, Oto knows this will be troublesome. Kori and the others feel the energy and feel like Fumiko is almost as powerful as Izanagi. Kori quickly runs up to the barrier and begins bashing it with his fist.

"Again, help me" Kori thought.

"Again, we have already made a pact, is this another favour you will owe me".

"Sure, just lend me your magical energy so I can destroy this damn barrier".

"Very well then, two favours will do me".

Kori's eyes glow red as his red aura destroys the magical barrier; Silva feels shivers as he can see how crazy Kori's red magical energy truly is.

"How does he have such immense magical power, his energy does not even belong to him, as if he was harbouring a demon inside him" Silva thought.

"Wow very cool Kori you took out that barrier like it was nothing," said Aithne.

"Why thank you" said Kori as he smiles with his thumb up.

"Let's not get cocky come on, lets head up the stairs and find out who we are defeating," said David.

Inside the room, Fumiko steps forward melting some of the floor with just her footsteps. Oto steps back and tries to figure out a plan to use his sound magic to get past her defences. He teleports above her placing both his hands facing her, he shoots a sound shock wave directly at her, she looks up with her glowing, yellow-coloured eyes and the wave shatters and blows Oto back a few metres.

"What the hell?" he said.

Oto uses his speed to get around Fumiko, he goes to punch her in the back but as his fists get close to her, they begin to burn up, he pulls back and gets to a safe distance.

"How are you doing this?" he asked.

"I control anything hot; I have three elements within me, magma, fire and heat, my magical energy acts as heat so anything that comes close to me will burn to ash".

Kori and the others head to the top of the stairs, they get to the door that asks as the control room for Brume tower. He opens the door slightly and peaks through, he senses dark magic from within. They walk in and are greeted by a man stood looking out the window at the end of the room.

"The volcano is still active, imagine it goes off, the devastation it would cause Loch would be horrible" he said.

"I don't think so, we are here to stop whatever you are doing and to bring you back with us for questioning," said Kori.

"My name is Kyoufu, I am shocked you beat all my followers, how sad, but it would seem you also broke my seal, just what magic do you use?".

Kyoufu

12 - Absolute

Kori steps forward, points at Kyoufu, "I will defeat you" he said with confidence.

"Defeat me, boy I am in multiple leagues higher than you, an ant inside my farm".

Kori swipes his arm and a huge branch shoot from the ground and smashes Kyoufu through the wall.

"His magic has improved" Silva thought.

Kyoufu appears behind Kori, blood squirts from Kori's chest as he falls to the ground face first. Silva and the others are in shock, the branch looked like it hit him, but he used a form of illusion magic to make it seem that he was hit to distract Kori. David looks at Kyoufu and sees he has a steel katana appear from his elbow.

"Be careful everyone, this guy uses a form of steel magic, he must have created the katana from his flesh" David warns.

"Correct, I use steel magic, my whole body can become a weapon, now who is next?".

Silva and David rush him, they use enhanced speed magic to throw multiple kicks and punches, Kyoufu's speed magic is greater, he manages to dodge every attack thrown at him. His fist turns into steel as the sheen from his fist catches the eye of Silva. He moves quick as he smashes Silva in the ribs with his fist, sending him flying through the door into the staircase.

David covers his hand in ice as he manages to punch Kyoufu in the face, the ice shatters as he turns his right side of the face steel to protect himself from the impact.

Aithne runs to Kori to check on him, she sees he has a big gash down the centre of his chest as blood stains his green top. She places her hand on his chest and uses heat magic to close the wound up. Kori opens his eyes and looks and sees David fighting with Kyoufu. He sits up and places his hand on his chest.

"Thank you" he said.

Aithne smiles and Kori stands on his feet, "let's help David" he said.

The two rushes in, Kyoufu sees this and turns both hands steel. Aithne uses fire magic to throw a huge fire ball at him, he blocks with his hand, steam appears and blocks some of his vision, through the steam Kori rushes through it and headbutts the exposed part of Kyoufu's face knocking him back a few steps.

"There we go a bit of a challenge I like it" Kyoufu said as he grins with excitement.

David summons an ice sword through his hand, he goes for a quick slice at Kyoufu's neck, he quickly leans back and does a back flip a few metres away from them.

Silva appears on the roof just above him and uses wind blast the hit Kyoufu to his knees, Kori uses wood magic to wrap vines around his arms to pull him closer to the ground. David jumps high into the air and creates a huge ice hammer and smashes Kyoufu in the back with a great impact cracking the floor below Kyoufu.

"Nice combo, shame you all are very weak" he said, "now let me show you a some of my true power".

Kyoufu releases his magical energy creating an immense atmosphere. His whole body turns to steel as he stands and tears the vines from his arms. He teleports behind Aithne and smashes her in her side with both his fists knocking her flying into a wall. David turns shocked as he goes for an attack, but Kyoufu is fast to react and stabs David through the stomach with a created blade from his fist, he then jump kicks David sending him through the window of the tower. Silva and Kori attack him, they both begin to release a magical attack, but it is stops as Kyoufu appears in the middle of them, he clotheslines them very hard as they smash into the ground.

"Lightwork..." he muttered.

He powers down as he is victorious, he walks over to the window and looks to the volcano.

"I am absolute" he said so gently.

Kori looks up at the sealing, his wound opened up from Kyoufu's attack, his vision becomes blurred as he can feel deaths door knocking.

"Is this how I die, how pathetic" he thought to himself, "I am too weak, I let my comrades get hurt, I cannot protect anyone".

"Switch" the voice in his head said.

Kyoufu feels a horrible magical energy appear behind him, he turns and sees Kori standing with a red aura surrounding him.

"You want more?" he asked.

Kori turns and he glares at Kyoufu with glowing red eyes, Kori grins at him.

"Finally, I have control" Kori said.

"Control, I think I may have hit you a bit hard, you are sprouting nonsense" Kyoufu said.

"Who do you think you speaking to human?" Kori asked.

"Who are you? The boy I beat had a weak aura; this aura is different".

"You can call me Okifumi, I am the one who is absolute, I am justice, I am a god".

"Okifumi, never heard of you".

Okifumi steps in front of Kyoufu faster than the eye can see, Kyoufu is shocked as Okifumi puts the palm of his hand on Kyoufu's face and teleport him above the volcano, he throws Kyoufu at high speed into the rocky peak of the volcano. Kyoufu sits up as blood drips from his mouth.

"The hell" he said.

Okifumi teleport in front of Kyoufu and looks at him while laughing.

"What's the matter? Can you not keep up is your human brain not capable" Okifumi gloats.

Kyoufu looks at Kori's chest and sees that it has completely healed.

"How is this possible?" he asked.

"Damn I healed this kids chest, ah well, this is my body now".

Kyoufu begins to feel fear, he tries to power up his magical energy but is stops as Okifumi raises his hand. Kyoufu begins to levitate, he is unable to move his body or even speak.

"You humans are so easy to kill, your downfall is being full of blood, one of my magical elements is blood magic, I can control other people's blood, let me show you".

The right arm of Kyoufu begins to bubble then suddenly it explodes as blood splatters all over the rocky floor.

"See, I destroyed your arm with such ease, I can increase, decrease or even extract blood with my magic, what shall I destroy next, or maybe I can do this".

Okifumi waves his hand around as high speed, wherever he waves his hand Kyoufu flies to, he smashes him in the ground over fifty times, breaking all the bones in his body.

"Switch" Okifumi hears Kori's voice in his head, he had a shocked look upon his face.

"How the hell?" he questioned; the red eyes turned back to green.

Kyoufu is released and falls to the ground unconscious.

"You listen to me, never take over again or I will not help you" Kori angrily said.

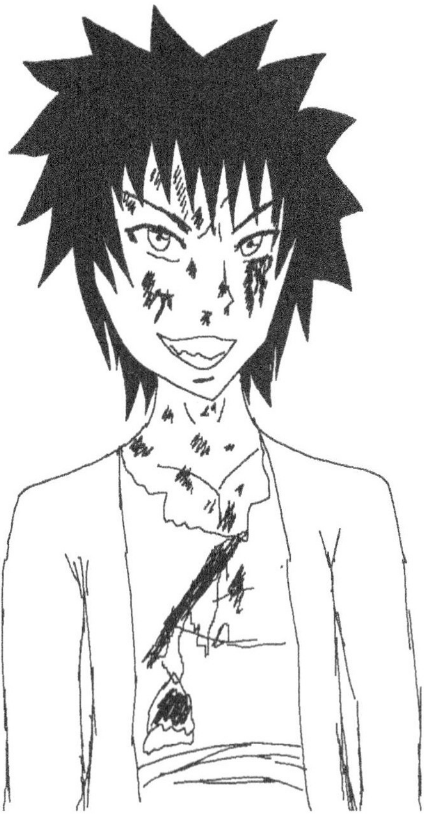

13 – Success

In the towers third floor, Oto is knocked out with burn injuries all over his body, Fumiko walks away to go check on her underlings. She reaches the top floor and sees that Aithne and Silva are on the floor knocked out from their injuries. She rushes over and sees that they are still alive, she uses teleportation magic to teleport them outside in from of Brume Tower where Luna and Kaito were waiting.

"Fumiko sensei," said Luna.

"Luna, give them these liquids it is an elixir with healing magic within" she sees David, he limps over holding his side.

"I'm sorry Fumiko sensei we failed" he said.

"Where is Kori? He was not upstairs" she asked.

"He wasn't upstairs, he was fighting alongside us" David said.

Fumiko closes her eyes and senses Kori; she looks up and sees his magical energy is coming from the top of the volcano.

"Wait here" she said, she teleports on top of the volcano right behind Kori.

Kori turns and sees Fumiko; she smiles as he is safe but looks at Kyoufu and is confused.

"Kyoufu the steel demon, was he in charge of this raid on Brume tower?".

"Yes, he was the leader" Kori said.

"What happened to him?".

"I am not sure; it is as if this voice in my head took over my body and defeated him".

"A voice, what is he talking about?" she thought.

She walks over to Kyoufu she sees he is still breathing; she stands and places her finger on her chin as she thinks.

"Kori seems to be unhurt which is strange, I will have to take Kyoufu back for questioning" she thought.

Fumiko places her hand on the back of Kyoufu and tells Kori to grab her hand, she teleports them down to the others. Everyone looks shocked as they witness Kyoufu looking a bloody mess with one arm missing.

"Okay, I see the elixir worked, is everyone feeling a bit better?" she asked.

"Yeah, it healed my wound thank you Fumiko sensei," said Aithne.

"Right, everyone, lets head back, we will take Kyoufu with us for questioning on his attempt to take Brume Tower, we will have to walk as I can only teleport a certain amount of people, David you carry him please".

Everyone heads back to Loch Academy, Fumiko takes Kyoufu to the Loch Warrior magic centre to be healed. Kori sits him his room thinking about how Okifumi took over his body by saying switch.

Kyoufu who is still out cold is placed in the dungeons as two guards wait for him to wake up, Fumiko heads to Master Ichiro's office to give him a report on the mission.

"Fumiko welcome back, I take it the mission was a success" he said.

"We defeated everyone at Brume Tower and captured the leader of the raid, the mission was a success".

"Very good, a high-level magic user like Kyoufu defeated is impressive well done for defeating him Fumiko".

"Master, it was not me who defeated Kyoufu, it was first year Kori Tenkai who defeated him".

"Kori Tenkai, a first year, but how, Kyoufu is a grand loch warrior level threat".

"I do not understand it either, Kori said he cannot remember beating him and that he heard a voice in his head, then the next he was standing over Kyoufu".

"A voice in his head, how bizarre" Ichiro stand from his chair, "I do remember Izanagi telling him he has a strange power and aura within him, we must keep an eye on him as this voice could be a danger to us all especially if this strange voice can take over his body to the point, he can defeat a grand loch warrior threat".

"Yes master, I will keep an eye on him until Izanagi gets back from his mission".

Ichiro dismisses Fumiko and sits down in his huge chair; he looks up at the light and begins to think this may cause some trouble down the line.

Nightfall arises, Kaito is in the combat ground, he stands still in the silence. He releases his magical energy glowing in an yellow aura, he concentrates hard as he releases electric orbs from his body, he sends them flying exploding in the air.

"I got embarrassed on that mission, Kori and Silva won their matches while I got beat up, I am sick of being weak, I will not fail again" Kaito thought to himself.

"Practice I see" Kaito turns and see Silva behind him in shorts and t shirt.

"Silva, what are you doing here?" Kaito curiously asked.

"I came to train also, you may have been beaten but I couldn't do anything against the leader, I need to get stronger so I can compete with that little shit Kori".

"I see, then let's have a few sparring matches".

The day after, team Izanagi are to report to the main courtyard, they arrive and see a stage with a mic and other first years and second years.

"This is strange why is everyone else here?" Kori questioned.

"Maybe Master Ichiro wants to announce something, but if so, I only see first years and second years here, wonder why the third years are not here," said Silva.

"Look on stage, there is Enji and Fumiko sensei" Luna pointed out.

"Where is Izanagi sensei?" Kaito asked.

"Not sure let's go forward guys," said Kori.

They head forward and team Enji spot them, they walk over to greet them.

"Hey Kori, how's it going?" Drake asked.

"Not bad, do you know what this is about?".

"Master Ichiro has an announcement; I have no idea what about".

Team Fumiko come over to Kori, Aithne inspects him, Kori feels creeped out by it.

"How is your chest?" She asked.

"Decent, I have a scar, but you saved my life with your magnificent magic so thank you".

"You're welcome" she said with a big smile.

Kori looks up at David, he sees this and turns his head to not acknowledge Kori. Everyone stops talking as Master Ichiro walks to the centre of the stage.

"Welcome young Loch Warriors, I bet you are all wondering why I called you all here" said Ichiro, "I have an announcement, the King has requested we show off our academy by hosting a tournament, this tournament will consist of a bracket with all your names, you will one v one each other with the winner being promoted to Rank one Loch Warrior".

Everyone begins to talk, Kori smiles at this new challenge that has arises in front of him.

"The tournament will begin in a months' time, so make sure you all train very hard, showcase your magic and your skills as people will be watching this tournament very closely, the more publicity the higher work you will get in the future, so good luck to everyone".

"Yes!! I finally get to prove myself and become the strongest" Kori shouts.

Everyone glares at Kori, "hm maybe I should have kept that to myself..." Kori muttered.

"Fool" said David.

Everyone leaves the area as Kori walks the academy trying to find Izanagi so he can get some special training.

"Awe man, I can't find him anywhere".

Kori walks around the corner and bumps into someone, "sorry about that," said Kori.

Kori looks up and sees a man with slick back brown hair, he wears a long black jumper with the sleeves rolled up and a gold chain around his neck.

"Tell me your name kid" he said.

"Kori Tenkai, I am a first year".

"Nice to meet you, I am Namiyo, Rank Three Loch Warrior".

"Rank three that is right below Grand Loch Warrior, you must be strong".

"Indeed, I am strong, what are your goals, Kori?".

"I am going to become the strongest Loch Warrior".

"Right well aren't you ambitious, well I best get going, I have a mission".

He begins to walk away, Kori begins to think, if Izanagi is not about maybe he can train him.

"Wait" Kori said.

"What is it?".

"Izanagi Sensei is not around; will you be able to train me for the upcoming tournament".

"Izanagi, so he is the leader of your squad?".

"Yeah, do you two know each other?".

"Izanagi was my sensei when I was in the academy, he taught me a lot, like I am strong, but he is in a different league to me if not a different league than any Loch Warrior in history".

"Wow, Izanagi sensei is the strongest loch warrior in history".

"He is, his magic is insane, but the answer to your question, I will train you, only because you are Izanagi's student".

"Wow thank you very much Namiyo Sensei".

"Sensei, the thought of someone calling me sensei brings a tear to my eye" he thought, "okay Kori, let's do this, follow me on the road to being the strongest".

"Yeah!!" Kori shouts.

Namiyo

14 – Namiyo

The sun rises over Loch Academy, Namiyo told Kori to be up early and ready to go on a mission with him. Kori waits beside a small tree at the entrance to the academy, he leans against the tree trying not to fall asleep.

"This is way too early, I am tired" Kori thought to himself.

Namiyo teleports in front of Kori, "morning kiddo".

"Morning, so what type of mission are we going on?".

"This is a high ranked mission; it is nothing I cannot handle but you want training so coming along, maybe you can learn a thing or two".

"Thank you, learning from a rank three Loch warrior will be great experience for me, plus all the others are training hard, I want to train hard and learn new things too".

"Good, then let's get going, we have a long walk ahead, we are going to Anthem City".

"Anthem City, that city is huge".

"It is, we have a client their so let's get moving".

Anthem City was located in the centre of Loch, it was a long fifteen hours walk, Kori and Namiyo occasionally stopped to do some training for Kori.

They stop next to a small lake; Namiyo puts down his backpack and is ready to teach Kori a few things.

"Right, magic energy control is key, show me how you would increase your magical energy".

Kori begins to focus; white aura surrounded him as he releases a large amount of magical energy.

"He knows how to raise his energy, but does he know how to maintain it" Namiyo thought.

"Okay Kori, now maintain this level of energy".

Kori stops powering up and tries to keep his magical energy at a steady high but struggles as his magical energy begins to get less powerful.

"I see, you can raise your energy for powerful attacks but then you gas out easily, maintaining a large amount of magical energy and using attacks means you can fight for much longer, on this mission I want you to only focus of keeping your magical energy at a steady pace that way your attacks can be more effective".

"So that is why when I fight, I run out of magical energy quite fast".

"Yes, if you can't control your magical energy then you will lose more battles a lot often so if this mission goes sideways then watch how I battle".

They set off again and walk all the way to Anthem City, the city was huge, buildings were high and everywhere, it was full of life as loads of people were walking, working, and living.

"Wow Namiyo sensei this city looks well busy".

"Well, it is the second largest city in Loch the first being Loch Kingdom, we need to head to find a man named Stephen".

Kori is wondering who Stephen is, Namiyo begins walking Kori quickly follows behind. They walk towards a small building, Namiyo bangs on the door. The door slightly opens with an old man peeking through.

"Who is it?" the old man asked.

"Namiyo, I am a Loch Warrior, are you Stephen?".

He opens the door, "I am, thank you for coming, please come inside".

Stephen sits down at his dining table, Kori and Namiyo sit across from him.

"So, Stephen, I understand you want to report a kidnapping?" Namiyo asked.

"Yes, my daughter she is only fourteen, she was kidnapped by Jin Tanaka, he is a gang leader of the most powerful gang in Loch".

"A gang leader?" Kori questioned.

"Jin Tanaka is not only a gang member, but he is also a prolific magical energy user, now tell me why he would kidnap your daughter?" Namiyo asked.

"Okay, I will explain, I use to be a part of Jin's gang the Crimson Knifes, I left, and Jin did not agree with it so he took my daughter to punish me, can you help me or not?".

"Do not worry, I will get your daughter back, now I need information as to where I can find Jin".

"North of the city there is an old warehouse, that is where the crimson knifes operate, but be careful it is very heavily guarded".

"Do not worry, I am Namiyo the rank three loch warrior, I got this and I have my little apprentice with me, we got this, see you soon".

Namiyo and Kori leave and head up the road north.

"Namiyo Sensei, what is the game plan?".

"We just go in their beat them all up get his daughter and deliver her to Stephen, then we can go for food before we head back to the academy".

"Oh, I was expecting we sneak around but if you wanna go in guns blazing I am all for it".

"Don't worry, we do not need to sneak, I am powerful, and these guys are just clowns".

They reach a metal fence that surrounds a big grey warehouse, they spot men stood outside the entrance, Namiyo jumps over the fence and struts all the way to the men outside.

"Wait right there, what business do you have?" one of the men said.

"Shut up, is Jin in today?" Namiyo asked.

"Leave now".

Namiyo laughs as he smashes them both with a water beam using water magic, they blast through the door and land in front of a meeting the gang seems to be having.

Namiyo and Kori walk in, the gang consists of twenty men, they check on the two knocked out men and look at Namiyo and Kori with rage.

"Which one of you idiots is Jin?" Namiyo asked.

A man in a long black coat walks forward, he had a red Mohawk and a scar on his right eye.

"I am Jin, you are coming here is a declaration of war".

"War, you do not want a war with me, I would destroy you all, now give Stephen his daughter back".

"I don't know what you are talking about, who the hell is Stephen?" Jin questioned.

"Don't play stupid he used to be a member of your little club; he said you took his daughter to get revenge on his leaving".

"I am sorry, but I do not know a Stephen, so you are wasting your time here".

"Scumbags like him usually lie, but looking at his eyes I can tell he is telling the truth" Namiyo thought.

Jin spots someone at the hole in the wall that Namiyo created, a silhouette of a man. Namiyo turns around and feels the persons magical energy. The ground begins to shake as magical energy can be felt from above. A large rock falls from the sky and smashes into the warehouse creating a loud explosion. A huge smoke cloud covers the entire area. As the smoke clears, the meteor is revealed, it was huge but stood still as a magical barrier stopped it. Kori looks to

Namiyo and sees he stopped the meteor with his magical energy, Kori was shocked.

"Namiyo sensei your magical energy is amazing," said Kori.

"It's no issue, it would seem that Stephen tricked us all".

"Wait how do you know that was Stephen?".

"I sensed the same magical energy when I first met him, now just give me a second".

Namiyo releases a water piercing attack and a million water pins bisect the meteor breaking it into tiny little pieces.

"Listen, I do not know you, but whoever this Stephen is be careful," said Jin.

"We will, come on Kori, let's go after him".

Kori and Namiyo leave, Namiyo remembers the man went left, so they head left which led to a forest, they speed into the forest in hopes of catching him.

"Kori, we head left, I sense magical energy," said Namiyo.

They launch from branch to branch as they head left, Kori sees a man with a long red jacket walking. They jump over the man and land right in front of him.

"Hold it right there, tell me what your real name is and what was the purpose of summoning me for a mission?" Namiyo asked.

"Ha ha ha, my name is Kazan, I am an assassin for the dark kingdom".

"Assassin, who sent you?".

"Master Rain wanted me to eliminate you, he thinks you are dangerous in his plans for the dark kingdom as you have the potential to be stronger than Izanagi".

"So, Rain is scared of me how cute".

"Not in that sense if he wanted to, he could kill you with ease, I do not see you as a threat, your magic is inferior to mine".

"Then, why not test our strength, after I am done with you, I will be bringing you back to Loch Kingdom to be imprisoned".

"Namiyo sensei is so cool" Kori thought.

"Kori, go and wait by that tree, I want you to spectate me and learn by just feeling my magical energy".

Kori heads by the tree and leans beside it, he focuses and sees that Namiyo is beginning to power up. Kazan teleports in front of Namiyo and quickly sidekicks him. Namiyo blocks with his left arm and sends Kazan flying with a water cannon from his hand. Kazan lands on a high tree branch looking down at Namiyo. Kazan creates flaming meteors from his hands and shoots them at Namiyo. The meteors come in fast, Namiyo quickly reacts by using magical forcefield to block them, they hit the forcefield instantly blowing up.

"His defence is pretty solid; I may need to turn it up a bit" Kazan thought.

Namiyo uses water piercer and shoots multiple sharp water shaped pins at Kazan, he leaps of the branch and spins trying to dodge but a pin shoot though his thigh, Kazan lands on the ground and looks to his leg as bloods drizzles down. He smirks and goes to test Namiyo's close combat. He dashes forward throwing punches and kicks, Namiyo has no issue as he does the same, the ground below the begins to crack as each connection shakes the ground.

"They are both evenly strong, come on Namiyo sensei beat him" Kori thought to himself.

Namiyo raises his hand causing a huge water cannon to shoot from the ground smashing Kazan in the stomach and raising him into the sky. Namiyo teleports behind Kazan and clubs him in the back, sending him flying into the ground. Namiyo lands and uses magical energy to blow away the dust cloud. Kazan is hurt as he is kneeling on the ground.

"Dammit, looks like I will have to use that technique..." Kazan muttered.

"Yeah, Namiyo sensei is doing it, you won!!" Kori shouted.

"Something is off, this was too easy" Namiyo thought.

Kazan looks at Namiyo as he stands back up, he smirks, "Shinka..." he said.

"Huh, he knows that" Namiyo worryingly said.

"Shinka, what is that?" Kori wondered.

Kazan is engulfed in magical aura as his magical energy is immense. Namiyo jumps back and stands in front of Kori protecting him for what is about to happen.

Kazan's red aura dimmers as it surrounded his outer body, his hair was black and red and spiked up, his arms were covered in red rock and his legs were covered in black rock.

"Namiyo sensei what did he just do?" Kori asked.

"He used Shinka, only strong magic users can use that move, it is magical evolution, it doubles your magical energy and transforms you depending on what magical element you have, his was meteors which mean his defence has become much higher".

"Shinka, damn, looks like we are in trouble" Kori thought.

Kazan within an instant punches Namiyo in the chest and unleashes an explosion sending Namiyo flying through multiple trees, Kori looks behind and shouts Namiyo. He turns and sees Kazan looking directly at him with a smirk.

"Are you trembling kid? you should be" Kazan said.

Kori powers his magical energy and stands in a fighting stance.

"Bring it on" Kori said.

Kori uses wood magic to control branches from the surrounding trees, they shoot towards Kazan and disintegrate, the aura from Kazan is that strong the heat from it was just like taking a bath in lava. Kazan smashes his huge rocky hand down upon Kori, Namiyo appears and blocks the strike with his hands. Kori quickly sends vines to wrap around Kazan's legs. Namiyo pushes Kazan's hands up leaving his body exposed. He water cannons Kazan sending him flying backwards but he stops by digging his feet into the ground.

"Not bad, but there is no way you can keep up with my Shinka form," said Kazan.

"Well looks like I have to play by your book" said Namiyo, "Shinka" he said so gently.

Kazan is stunned as Namiyo uses Shinka, his aura blinding him with him being covered in a blue and white aura, the transformation is complete as the blue aura surrounds Namiyo, his hair turn light blue with his eyes glowing blue, his whole body was covered in water that was shaped like knight's armour.

"Wow" said Kori.

The rocks surrounding Kazan's arms glow as he rushes in, swinging wildly, Namiyo dodges with ease and creates a long lance, Kazan punches the tip of the lance, but his boulders are destroyed. Namiyo spins and thrusts the lance through the chest of Kazan and unleashes a huge water cannon sending Kazan flying through the trees and into a cliff, Kazan turns back to normal as he falls to the ground unconscious. Namiyo powers down and sticks his thumbs up at Kori.

"That was insane your power is incredible," said Kori.

"Thanks, and do not forget I controlled my magical energy so that I still have reserves, meaning I could easily hold that form for quite a long time".

"I see, sensei do you think I could learn Shinka?".

"Shinka is a transformation that only the elite magic users can use, there is no doubt you cannot learn it but it will take years of training before you could reach that level".

Kazan lays face down on the dusty surface, he looks up and sees a black shadow on the floor. He begins to sweat and tremble as the shadow begins to form of the ground. Namiyo and Kori walk towards and see the shadow, Namiyo stops as he senses huge magical energy. The shadow was a black silhouette of a man with long hair.

"M-master Rain, please I can explain," said Kazan.

The shadow points the palm of the hand towards Kazan and releases a curse causing Kazan to inflate and explode black sludge all over the rocks and ground. The shadow turn to Kori and Namiyo with a face with no emotion, the shadow disappears without a trace.

"Who was that?" Kori wondered.

"That was Rain, I will never forget his dark forbidden magic".

"Dark magic?"

"Yeah, Rain was on the level of Izanagi when he was a Loch Warrior, but he was obsessed with power and learnt dark magic which is forbidden in Loch law, that is why he left and went to the dark kingdom".

"I see, so he is the man pulling the strings within the dark kingdom".

"Yeah, it is a shame he killed Kazan we could have gotten great intel from him, lets head back and do some training for you".

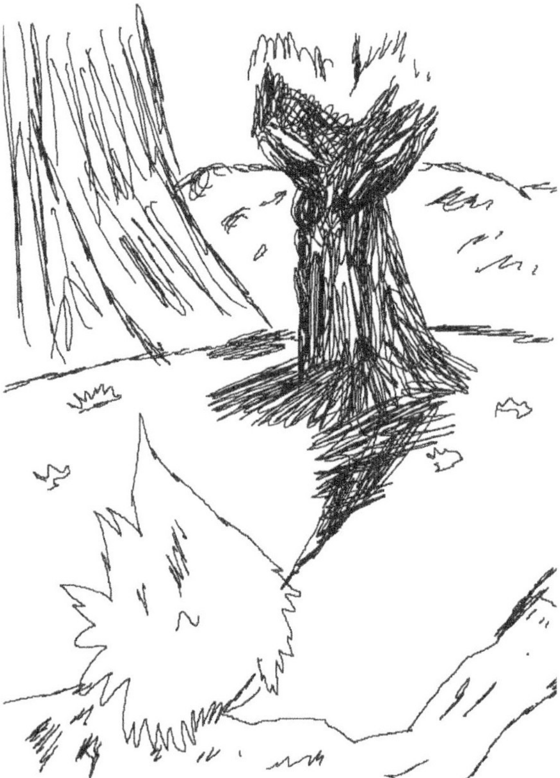

15 – Preparation

Kori and Namiyo are back at the academy, Kori heads to his room to get some sleep while Namiyo heads to Ichiro to report what happened on his mission.

"So, there is a level that is beyond the average magic user, Shinka, I cannot wait to learn it" Kori thought to himself.

Kori hears a knock on his door, he wonders who it is, so he heads over and opens the door, it was Athine.

"Hey Kori, just wondering" she said as she was blushing.

"What's up?" Kori asked.

"Do you want to train tomorrow?" she asked.

"Yeah sure, your magic is great so training with you would help me a lot thank you," said Kori.

"Good, good well see you tomorrow" she said with a big smile, she runs off.

"That was strange, but I have a training partner now which is good, I wonder how everyone else's training is going" Kori thought.

Back at Ichiro's office Namiyo has summoned Fumiko and Enji, "why have you summoned us, Namiyo? Fumiko asked.

"I went on a mission to Anthem City, there I was tricked by a man, he tried to kill me and a gang".

"A man tricked you?" Enji questioned.

"Yes, so he asked for help to take out a gang who kidnapped his daughter, but he was lying, he was assigned a task to assassinate me by the dark kingdom, after I defeated this man Rain showed himself and eliminated him".

"Rain actually showed himself?" Fumiko asked.

"Yes, it would seem he is making his move, he is targeting high level Loch warriors".

"If this is the case then should you not cancel the tournament," said Enji.

"No, this is the perfect opportunity to lure the dark kingdom, we will place more high-level loch warriors at the tournament," said Ichiro.

"Master is right, is Izanagi back from his mission yet?" Namiyo asked.

"Not yet, but he should be back in time for the tournament" Ichiro stated.

"Well let's be extra careful, protecting the students is number one priority," said Fumiko.

"As of now, all missions will be cancelled until the tournament is concluded, who knows which mission could be a lure to attack us so for now on we will protect the kingdom and the academy," said Ichiro.

"Understood master" everyone said.

The morning arrives and Kori is up very early to go eat breakfast, he heads to the cafeteria. He sees David is in line picking his breakfast, Kori walks up behind with, David notices this and gives him an evil stare.

"Hey there Dave," said Kori.

"It's David you midget, how is your training going?".

"Not bad, I am training with Athine today so should be a good session, bout yourself?".

"You do not need to know about my training, just know if we face each other in the tournament, I will win".

"Bring it on" said Kori, he was excited by David's comments.

Kori and David grab their breakfast and head in opposite directions, Kori eats on a bench outside while he waits for Athine to arrive.

"Man, I haven't seen Silva, Kaito and Luna in two days I wonder if they are training" Kori wondered.

"Hey Kori" said Aithne, she runs up to him.

"Hey, so what training should we do today?".

"Hm not too sure, we could work on our magic control or practice hand to hand combat," said Aithne.

"How about you two train with me, I can't have my young student falling behind in the tournament," said Namiyo.

Kori and Aithne turn and see Namiyo walking up to them.

"Oh Namiyo Sensei, how did the meeting go?" Kori asked.

"Not too bad, so who is this your girlfriend?".

"G-girlfriend..." Aithne nervously said.

"Hm I am not too sure; she is a girl and my friend, so I guess so".

Aithne punches Kori in the back of the head, "I am just your friend stupid".

"Ha well, I guess you are clueless, nether the less, let us head into the forest and do some training," said Namiyo.

They head into the forest where Namiyo shows them a square battle ground within the forest trees.

"Wow what is this place?" Kori asked.

"This is where the first Loch Warrior held a tournament three hundred years ago, I figured this will be the perfect place to do some training" Namiyo explained.

"Merrick created this place?" Kori asked.

"Yes, Merrick did all of his training here, now let us begin with you two vs me, come at me with all you have".

"Wait you want us to fight you?" Aithne asked.

"Yes, show me you best attacks, this way I will know what you need to do to improve".

Kori and Aithne stand in a fighting stance, they both move fast at Namiyo. Aithne jumps and uses a fire fist, Namiyo leans his head left to dodge the attack, Kori quickly roundhouse kicks him In the neck, but it had no effect as Namiyo uses water shock, a dome of water releases from his body knocking Aithne and Kori back.

"Aithne, use your lava release to counter his water, I will wrap him up then use an offence attack" Kori said.

"Right".

Aithne uses Lava wave to create a wave of lava to cover Namiyo, he uses force field to block it, as the steam from the lava fogs up the area, Kori uses vines to shoot from the ground within his barrier to tie him up from the legs to the waist.

"Nice battle IQ Kori" Namiyo thought.

Kori uses magic drain by having the vines absorb magical energy from Namiyo. Namiyo looked shocked and impressed at the same time. The barrier vanishes and Aithne fires up her fists as she charges in to attack Namiyo with a barrage of fire punches. Namiyo points to the sky and summons a huge cloud, he muttered the word cannon cloud and from within the cloud eight water cannons shoot down upon Athine. Kori grabs her and carries her away from the attack.

"Thanks, what is our plan now, his defence is too strong," said Aithne.

"Not too sure, we may have to both go all out use our best attacks".

Kori and Aithne stand side by side, they power up their magical energy, Namiyo watches with a grin of excitement, he cannot believe how amazing their magical energy is. Kori teleports in front of Namiyo and power punches him, Namiyo blocks with one hand, Aithne appears above him and with both hands shoot a huge fire blast causing a huge explosion. Namiyo throws Kori up in the air and teleports above them both.

"Damn, think Kori, think" Kori thought. Namiyo creates a huge water sphere and launches it down at Aithne and Kori, the ground explodes with the aftershock destroying the surrounding trees.

"Wait, I think I may have gone a bit hard on them" said Namiyo as he lands on his feet.

The smoke clears and to Namiyo's surprise, Kori used a defence technique a green orb surrounded him and Aithne.

"That was a close one, good job Kori" said Athine.

"This kid is surprising; he may one day surpass me or even Izanagi".

David Drakai

16 – Round One

The day of the tournament has arrived, the first match will begin at lunch time but first things first and that is the bracket draw. All first years and second years arrive in the middle of the fight arena. The arena was a huge Colosseum the middle was filled with sand surrounded by the thousands of seats. Kori was overjoyed as he was shaking with excitement to compete in front of everyone.

"Okay everyone, welcome the tournament will begin after lunch we will have three battles today and it will be in front of the other upper students, loch warriors and the people of Loch Kingdom, so make sure you fight to the best of your ability," said Ichiro.

"The bracket will appear on the huge board behind me, the first fight will start from the left all the way to the right, so good luck as the people of Loch Kingdom will be watching".

The board was white nothing on it, a man with glasses walks up to the board and points his finger, yellow sparkles splashed onto the board revealing a names and match ups.

Everyone looks and reads carefully, the first match is Kaito Mizuno vs David Drakai, second match Kori Tenkai vs Drake Xero, third match Luna Evergrande vs Aithne Agni, fourth match Silva Mainz vs Seiji Kaneko, fifth match Eledro vs

Jin Tenchi, sixth match Junji Kutsuki vs Akira Yami, seventh match Scarlett Mainz vs Heidi Sye and eighth and final match for round one is Yumar vs Atticus.

Kori cheers as he is excited to fight against Drake, he looks to Drake and gives him a thumbs up, Drake nervously laughs, "Kori in the first round just my luck" he thought.

A few hours pass by Kori enters the stadium and heads to the waiting rooms, he sees Silva and Kaito, "hey guys, I hope you are ready to put on a show," said Kori.

"This is scary look at this" said Kaito.

Kaito shows Kori the arch into the stadium and shows the huge crowd there must be one thousand people here. Kori senses high magical energy and looks up and sees a VIP box up top and sees XOF and other Grand loch warriors watching from above.

"I cannot believe this many people are here to see us; I can't wait to show them my magic".

David walks into the room and Kaito gives him an evil glare. Kori runs up to him, "Dave, Dave how are you?" he asked.

"Ugh, you are so annoying, you better win your match cause in the second round I will destroy you," said David.

"That sounds like fun, do not worry about me, I will give it my all against Drake".

The first match is about to begin, Kori and friends watch from the stands, Kaito and David walk to the ring, a grey square in the middle of the arena, the crowd roars as they both walk up the steps and face each other. Enji is the referee he stands outside the ring.

"Okay guys, a clean fight, show off your abilities and have fun, if I see that one of you is about to be seriously hurt, I will intervene so no killing okay," said Enji.

"Kaito Mizuno!! David Drakai!!, begin!!" Enji shouts.

Kaito uses his fast-lightning speed to appear in front of David, he throws a lightening fist towards the chest of David. David smirks and ice appears from the ground between Kaito and David, Kaito's lightening fist smashes into the ice. David jumps back and sends ice shards flying at Kaito who is forced to use lightening fist to smashes all the shards to pieces. The crowd cheers as the fast-paced match excites everyone.

"Wow Kaito must have trained hard his movement is insane," said Kori.

"He knew David is a defensive guy, so he focused on his speed and attack during training" Silva explained.

"Incredible, I wish I was the one fighting Kaito" Kori thought.

"He thinks fast, I need to move faster and hit him with something unpredictable" Kaito thought.

Kaito focuses his magical energy and instantly teleports, David is shocked and couldn't see where he teleported to. He looks up and sees Kaito flying down towards him, Kaito quickly smashes a lightning strike on the top of David's head causing an explosion.

Kori and Silva looked shocked as they watch on, a huge smoke cloud covers the ring. Kaito breathes heavy, that attack took quite a bit of magical energy to do. The smoke begins to clear, Kaito looks on to see if he was victorious with the attack, but ice was revealed through the smoke. The ice shatters and David stands unfazed by the hit.

"Is that all you got, how pathetic," said David.

Kaito feels rage at the words of David and charges in, he begins throwing punches, David uses his hands to block and push away the furious punches of Kaito. David grabs Kaito's hand and pulls him towards himself and delivers a huge punch to the stomach of Kaito, causing him to cough out blood. David throws him high up over the ring and sends an array of ice blocks flying at Kaito, each one smashing into the body, David shows off his speed and appears in the air over Kaito, he smashes Kaito in the face and sends him flying outside of the ring.

David lands on the edge of the ring looking down at an unconscious Kaito as he lay on the damaged floor.

"Your winner by ring out DAVID DRAKAI!!" Enji announced. The crowd claps and cheers for David, but he did not care, he walks away and back into the waiting room, he walks past an angry Kori.

"Hey, do not get cocky, when you face me, I will show you to not disrespect your comrades".

"Comrades, we are not comrades, you are a weakling, that is all there is to it," said David.

"Kori, just leave it, you are up next any way," said Silva.

"Yeah, you are right, I hope Kaito is okay".

Enji stands in the ring as the medical team carry away Kaito, "alright what a first match, are you all ready for the next match," said Enji.

Kori smirks and starts to walk out, "good luck Kori, I will be cheering you on," said Aithne.

Kori blushes, "thank you".

Drake and Kori walk out to the ring, Drake looks at the stands and sees XOF stood up looking down at him.

"You watch father, I will show you why I will surpass you" Drake thought.

Kori and Drake stand facing each other with smiles on their faces.

"Show me your magnificent magic Drake Xero," said Kori.

"I intend too," said Drake.

Luna arrives in the waiting room; she sees Kori is ready to fight.

"Don't worry, I can see Kori has improved," said Silva.

"Huh, what makes you think I am worried; I know Kori will win," said Luna.

"Kori Tenkai!!, Drake Xero!! BEGIN!!".

Drake sends three fire balls Kori's way, Kori jumps over them and is met with a fire punch to the face, he goes flying and stops onto the edge of the ring.

"Amazing..." Kori muttered.

"Wow your son is very impressive XOF," said Fumiko.

"No, he is too weak, he will never reach my level" XOF states.

Kori teleports in front of Drake's face, he steps back in shock as Kori gut punches him and touches the floor below him, vines sprout out wrapping around both arms of Drake. He tries to burn the vines away, but Kori flips back and sends a huge wooden log from the ground knocking Drake onto his back. Kori gives him no time to rest as he jumps very high into the air, he uses red lightening to cover his arm and flies down and strikes causing the arena to rumble. Kori knew Drake dodged and uses green orb to protect himself from a fire ball blast.

"Huh?" Drake was confused.

Athine laughs, "you go Kori, green orb is your perfect defence". Silva hears her, "Green orb, so Kori is using his magical energy to cover himself in a sphere to protect himself from magical attacks" Silva thought.

Drake breathes fire at Kori, as the flames get closer Kori laughs "I hope you are watching Dave". Kori breathes fire back at Drake and the flames collide heating up the arena.

"Wait what?" Silva said.

"Kori can use fire magic too, what a guy," said Aithne.

"Wood magic, lightening magic, Fire magic and blood magic, is this..." Ichiro mutters.

The flames disperse, Kori stands in front of Drake with a cheeky grin, Drake sighs and shrugs his shoulders.

"Impressive you can use fire magic, but the question is can you control it like me".

Drake covers his fists in fire and charges aggressively at Kori, he throws hard punches and Kori dodges but feels burns appearing on his skin.

"His fire magic keeps getting hotter even the steam from his fists is burning me, I need to end this quick" Kori thought.

Kori roundhouse kicks Drake in the chest sending him back a few steps, the determination of Drake is strong, he turns his flames into a whip and whips Kori on the right arm setting his right arm up in flames.

Kori tears off his right sleeve from his blue jacket and jumps high into the air. Drake turns his whip into a bow and pulls back a fire arrow to shoot. Kori smiles, he is impressed with Drake's magic.

"You are amazing Drake; your magic is incredibly cool" Kori thought.

Drake fires the fire arrow at Kori who teleports, Drake is shocked and looks around and cannot see Kori anywhere. Drake feels uneasy as he sweats, he has no time to think, he reckons Kori will launch a sneak attack, so he raises his hands into the air and slams them onto the arena floor sending a shock wave of flames to force Kori out of hiding. The flames vanish and still no sign of Kori, Drake looks up and spots a surge of red lightening.

"What the hell is that?" Drake muttered.

Kori flies down at speed greater than the speed of light as his hand is covered in red lightening, he chops Drake on the back of the neck causing the ground to rumble. Drake is shocked as he begin to lose consciousness as he falls to the ground.

The crowd is shocked also as they begin to clap for Kori, "the winner by KO, Kori Tenkai!!" Enji shouted.

Kori laughs and raises his fist in the air, "that is one step to becoming the best" Kori thought.

Kori heads back to the waiting room and is greeted by Silva, Luna, and Aithne.

"How did you learn fire magic?" Silva asked.

"Who cares how he learned it, congratulations Kori" said Athine.

"Thanks, ha ha, magic is a sauce from within, I think being a Tenkai has some part in it, I have no idea," said Kori.

"It is true, Drakai and Tenkai, both clans can possess more than one element" Luna explained.

"Hey Luna, we are up next good luck, I hope we tear the house down" Aithne said with a smile on her face.

"Err… yeah" said Luna, she looked nervous.

Aithne heads out first, Luna waits behind, she looked worried.

"Luna, you got this, your magic is special show everyone just who you are," said Kori.

"Yeah, your part of team Izanagi, that makes us comrades so do your best," said Silva.

Luna blushes and smiles, "thanks guys I will do my best".

Luna heads out and stands opposite Aithne, the two looked tense as they can see they are being watched by all.

"Aithne Agni and Luna Evergrande, BEGIN!!" Enji shouted.

Aithne quickly launches a fire ball at Luna, she dodges by jumping right, Aithne is very quick, she fire punches Luna in the gut and sends her flying to the edge of the ring.

"Damn, Aithne is too good, Luna needs to do something here or it is over," said Silva.

Aithne sucks in oxygen, Luna knows she will go for fire breath, she begins chanting in her head, Aithne unleashes a huge beam of fire from her mouth covering Luna in fire. The crowd gasps hoping for Luna to be okay, Kori smirks and Silva sees this.

"What's funny?" he asked.

"Just watch," said Kori.

The fire vanishes and Luna is covered in a green orb, the orb shatters like a brick smashing a window.

"A defensive shield, very impressive," said Aithne.

Luna holds her hand out and from a portal below a wooden staff levitates to Luna's hand.

"Let me show you, the power of my sisters". Luna sends crystal arrows from her staff, they fly at Aithne, she covers her face with her arms as she takes on the damage, the arrows shatter as they bounce of Aithne. She smiles as only small scratches show up from those arrows, she begins charging in, Luna quickly shoots a blue spirit Jellyfish her way, she backs up and jumps high into the sky, the Jellyfish follows like it has locked onto its target and will not stop following. Luna shoots more crystal arrows, but they miss, Aithne is confused it looked like she missed on purpose. Aithne creates a huge fire ball out of frustration and launches it at the Jellyfish causing a massive explosion within the arena.

"Damn that was Luna's best attack" said Silva, he was worried.

"You really think that blue haired witch can beat Aithne, you first years are so stupid," said Seiji.

"What did you say?" Silva turns with rage in his eyes, Kori puts his hand on Silva's chest.

"Let it go, you face him in the next round," said Kori.

Seiji smirks at Silva as he walks past very smug.

The smoke clears and Luna has lost sight of Aithne, she hears bangs on the ground around her. She turns and Aithne was moving at enhanced speed, Aithne with flames on her first smashes Luna in the face causing an explosion and Luna flying out of the ring and into a wall. Kori and Silva are shocked as they rush out of the waiting room to give her aid.

"Your winner Aithne Agni!!" Enji announced.

Silva leans down to check on the damage and sees Luna has passed out.

A medical team come out with a stretcher and ask Silva and Kori to step aside, they place her on the stretcher and begin to escort her to the medical room, one of the medical officers tell Silva and Kori she will be okay.

Kori and Silva head back into the waiting room, Silva looked really angry. Seiji walks past Silva; he turns his head slightly.

"You better not be weak like your teammate, got it" he said as he walks out.

"Let's get ready for the fourth match, coming to the ring we have another first-year vs second year, we have representing Team Fumiko, Seiji Kaneko and representing Team Izanagi, Silva Mainz!!" Enji announced to everyone.

Silva stands quiet and looking relaxed, Seiji smiles thinking this is a miss match, "you might as well call it Enji senpai, this kid is weak, he stands no chance".

Seiji turns his arms into steel, he clenches his fists tight and is ready to fight. Silva looks up with an expression of emptiness he points his finger and sends out a powerful tornado beam smashing Seiji and sending him crashing into the wall outside of the ring, the crowd is silent in shock.

"Erm. your winner Silva Mainz!!".

Silva puts his hands in his pockets and walks away, the crowd cheer for an impressive victory by Silva.

"That kid has excellent magic control; he has potential of being a grand loch warrior one day," said Ichiro.

Silva walks through the tunnel towards the waiting room and is passed by a muscular guy with a white jacket and bright green hair, Silva turns and feels uneasy at the guy's presence.

"Who the hell was that?" he thought.

He walks back in and heads to the stands to sit with Kori and watch the next match.

"What is the name of the guy with green hair?" Silva asked.

"I think he is called Eledro, why?".

"There is something weird about him, his magic feels sickly".

"The next match is Jin Tenchi and Eledro, both promising young loch warriors, begin!!".

Jin conjures lightening from his hands, he begins to create a ball of lightening. Eledro looked calm, he gazed at Jin with his pink eyes.

"Take this!!" Jin yelled... suddenly a gash on his chest appears blood squirts out as he cannot move, he falls backwards and out of the ring.

"How did he cut him?" Silva was confused.

Kori analyses Eledro's magical energy and sees a huge amount pulsating from his eyes.

"Is his eyes the source of the slash attack he just released, if so that power is crazy strong" Kori thought.

Eledro turns and as he is about to walk out of the ring he looks up and gazes upon Kori. Kori looks back and begins to sweat.

"Why is he looking at me?" Kori was so confused. The next round would be Junji vs Akira, Kori and Silva decide to miss this fight and head into the back to see how Luna and Kaito was doing. They both were in a bed asleep, Kori begins poking Kaito on the forehead.

"Hey what are you doing?" Silva asked in a quiet voice.

"Why are you whispering? Kaito has been asleep way too long".

Kori uses lightening magic to send a small shock onto Kaito, he jumps up very fast.

"What the hell Kori? I was enjoying my dream ya know..." said Kaito.

"Well, you are missing all the fights, but then again there is only two matches left for today".

"I have to go against that Aithne, her fire magic may be strong, but I will show her that Team Izanagi is no team to be messed with," said Silva.

"Hmm... I have never seen Silva so fired up" Kaito thought.

Kori and Silva head back to the stands, they see high speed wind magic, it felt like a tornado was spinning around the ring.

"Oh god, that is like your magic Silva" said Kori as he covers his face.

"That's my older sister Scarlett, we don't really talk".

"It looks like she is against that girl with purple hair, Heidi Sye".

Scarlett uses tornado vortex, a powerful beam of swirling wind magic locks onto Heidi, she tries using psychic magic to deflect the beam, it begins to move but the beam is too powerful and collides with Heidi sending her flying to the edge of the ring. Scarlett smirks as the edge Heidi is standing on crumbles causing Heidi to fall out of the ring.

"The winner Scarlett Mainz!!" Enji announces.

"Wow, that was crazy, is she smarter than you Silva?" Kori asked.

"Shut up you loser, let's go get something to eat, the second round begins in one hour and you are against that big oath".

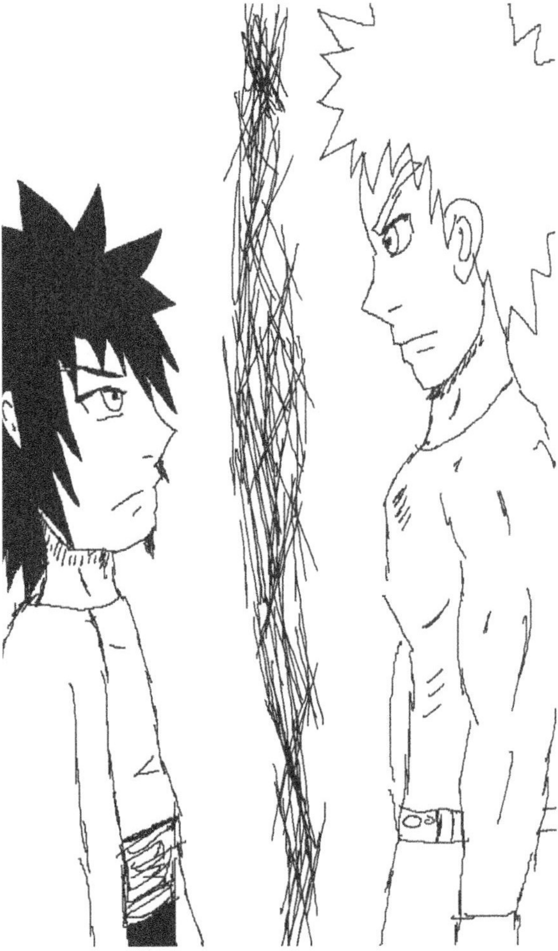

17 – Drakai and Tenkai

The crowd was roaring for the next round, an hour passes as Scarlett beats Heidi, the first match of the second round will be Kori Tenkai vs David Drakai. The grand loch warriors and upper ranks sit in the stands they are excited to watch this bout.

Kori stands at the entrance ready to make his way to the ring, David appears next to me, not even acknowledging that he is there.

"Good luck Dave," said Kori.

He ignores Kori and begins walking out to the ring, Kori quickly follows behind him. The crowd cheers, Kori is excited as he waves to the crowd.

Silva brings Kaito and they both sit up in the stands with Jin and Junji.

"Junji who won in your bout?" Silva asked.

"Erm it was me, I used Decay magic to decay the ring and eliminate Akira".

"I see…" Silva muttered, "what a strange guy" he thought.

"Come on Kori do not lose to him" said Kaito.

"I don't know, David is pretty much almost rank one level within the loch warrior rankings, his ice magic is too powerful," said Jin.

"Do not count Kori out, if anyone can beat David it is him," said Silva.

"It is time for the next round, please give a warm welcome to Kori Tenkai and David Drakai, now be ready, let us begin!!".

Kori teleports in front of David and leg kicks the side of David's head which is blocked by David's big hands, he grabs Kori's foot and launches him into the sky. He uses ice shards to launch at Kori who spins dodging the sharp edges of the ice shards, he lands on his feet and sends a sharp vine at David who ducks freezes the vine. David snaps it creating a long spear and charges at Kori. He thrusts the spear at high speed, Kori flips over and manages to kick David in the back of the head, they both managed to land on their feet. A cut appears on Kori's right cheek with a drop of blood dripping down, Kori smiles and turns to David.

"You are incredible David Drakai" he said.

David does not smile he feels creeped out by how much Kori is enjoying the battle, he crushes the spear into ice dust as he goes into a martial arts stance ready to show off his hand-to-hand combat skills. He speeds forward and hit David with a right kick which is blocked by David's elbow the impact of the kick cracks the stone ground below him. David goes for a punch which Kori bends backwards to dodge, Kori backflip kicks David in the face knocking him backwards and causing David to bleed from the lip.

David was furious as he releases a huge amount of magical energy, it was that large that the grand loch warriors were so invested while watching. Kori concentrates his magical energy; he knows David will prepare a strong attack.

"It all ends here; I will prove to you that I am the strongest and you are a no body," said David.

"You are wrong Dave; you think power is from loneliness when true power comes from the support and help of your comrades," said Kori.

"Iceberg slash!!" David yells.

"Routes of old!!" Kori yells.

David sends huge ice shards towards Kori while Kori's technique shoots huge tree routes from the ground both moves connect cracking the ring in half and shaking the stadium.

Both magical energy of Kori and David is running low, both moves cancelled each other out, they both run at each other ready for a final throw down. As they are about to punch each other a black shadow appears between the two. They both stop and a man with a pale face and long white hair appears from the shadow below himself.

"Who is that?" Ichiro asked.

The man casts incredibly fast spiralling portals below the feet of David and Kori, they both fall in, and the man vanishes through his own portal.

"Huh?" Silva looked shocked, suddenly a black portal appears below him, he begins to fall into the portal.

"Silva!!" Kaito yells.

"This is an emergency, all Grand Loch Warriors and grade 1's and above search the kingdom, find our Kori Tenkai and David Drakai at once" Ichiro instructed.

The room was made of black shiny bricks, from floor to walls to ceiling. Kori stands up and rubs his back side.

"Ouch my butt, where the hell are we?" Kori wondered.

"Not sure, but that guy had bad aura about him," said David.

Silva falls from the roof and lands on his back, he rolls his eyes as he sits up.

"Damn, looks like I will have back problems when I am older now" he said.

"David look" said Kori, he points towards the walls.

David turns and is shocked, he sees a banner of the dark kingdom on the walls.

"That's right...".

Kori, David, and Silva look forward to try and see who said that and on a black throne sits a man with long black hair and his eye colour was black.

"Welcome to my home, Kori Tenkai, David Drakai and Silva Mainz" he said, his voice was gentle, yet he had a sinister look upon his face.

Rain

18 – Rain

"Who are you?" David asked.

"Me, well is it not obvious?".

"No, you look like a creep," said Kori.

"My name is Rain; I am the leader of the Dark Kingdom".

Silva is furious, "leader…" he thought, out of rage he sends a gust of wind blades towards Rain. He smirks as he lifts a finger and the wind heads into the shadows on the floor from the pillars.

"That is no use, my shadows absorb all magical energy that is not natural," said Rain.

"What do you want with us?" Silva asked.

"You three have special magic energy I need, Kori with Blood Magic, David with Light magic and Silva with Dark Magic, I want your power, with that power I can take Loch for myself".

"What are you talking about, Kori's magic is wood, and Silva's is wind, I certainly cannot use Light magic," said David.

"Wait, the thing inside me, he knows how to use Blood Magic," said Kori.

"Correct, you have the soul of Okifumi inside you, one of the most powerful magic users in history, so I will take him from you".

Rain stands, Kori uses forcefield to protect David and Silva, shadow fragments bounce of the forcefield.

"Clever, you are a fast thinker, with the eyes of Okifumi you can see magical energy manifest, you saw that I was releasing magical energy to attack you three".

Kori begins to levitate; he is directed through the pillar and into the wall.

"Kori!!" Silva yells.

David turns around and sees a man with long spiky purple hair and glowing orange eyes.

"Looner Sye" said Silva.

"Sorry for the interruption master Rain, but we cannot have Okifumi manifest, he is too dangerous".

"Correct Looner, let us take out these two and place Kori into a cell below us, we will take his power later".

"Bring it on you bastards," said Silva.

Rain releases ten percent of his power creating a huge amount of black aura, the room becomes dark. David and Silva are stunned, they feel unease and have goosebumps all over their bodies.

"Damn I can't move" Silva thought.

Kori wakes up, he tries to move but his ribs are broken, he thinks it must have been from the pillars.

Rain creates a black orb from his hand, he points it directly at Silva and David.

"This is black death a ball that will destroy anything it touches, my advice to you two is to not dodge just accept your fate," said Rain.

"Crap this is bad, even Silva is frozen" David thought.

Rain launches black death, the orb flies at great speed, David grits his teeth and closes his eyes as the orb closes in on him and Silva.

The orb gets one metre away from David and Silva, a huge red lightning strike connects with it causing a massive explosion. The smoke clears and Kori appears in front of David and Silva, his eyes glowing red as he holds his damaged chest.

"Kori..." Silva muttered.

"Red coloured eyes, is it you Okifumi?" Rain asked.

"My name is Kori Tenkai, I will not let you harm my friends, understood you creepy looking arsehole".

"What? Impossible, how is this kid controlling the powers of the great Okifumi" Rain thought with a shocked look upon his face.

Silva and David stand by Kori's side, they both power up their magical energy ready to team up to take on Rain.

"I will annihilate you all, my next move is shadow rain, prepare yourselves" the tone in Rain's voice changed it was more menacing.

The roof becomes engulfed in darkness, the room trembles as the shadows become pointy.

"Damn, I need to use my defensive move to protect us all, but this magic, it is as if it does not follow the magical energy rule" Kori was thinking.

Rain laughs as he raises his arms to begin the shadow rain technique. Kori, Silva and David were worried. The side wall on the room explodes casting the shadow rain away as sunlight enters the room. Rain is shocked he pans his head left to see who has done this, even Kori and co were shocked.

"He he, you young Loch Warriors did well, let me take over".

Izanagi appears and walks into the room, he gives a thumbs up to Kori, Silva, and David with a cheeky smile.

"Izanagi, h-how did you find this place?" Rain asked.

"Oh Rain, I thought you was much smarter than this, such a shame you are a weak loser".

"Your arrogant bastard" Rain was furious at Izanagi calling him weak.

"I have been in Nortdrum, figuring out what the Dark Kingdom has been up to, I had to destroy a few of your pathetic bases but one of you minions told me that this was your main bases and as soon as I felt Kori's magical energy vanish from the academy stadium, I knew this would be the place you were keeping him and the others".

"You were always a pain in my side, I will end you here and now," said Rain.

"Don't be stupid we both know that I am the strongest and it would just end in your death," said Izanagi.

"Izanagi Sensei is so cool" Kori thought.

A guard is pissed that Izanagi insulted Rain, he pulls an axe and charges at Izanagi.

"Get lost" said Izanagi, he puts his hand out and the man is destroyed along with the left side of the building.

"This is the power of Izanagi, this is insane" David thought.

"You are right Izanagi, you are the strongest, so this time next month on the outskirts of Loch Kingdom, I will have magical users around five thousand, so prepare yourselves for a war," said Rain.

"A war…," said Silva.

"A war is not smart Rain, you are forgetting we have three other Grand Loch Warriors with great strength, it is a war that the Dark Kingdom will not win".

"Izanagi Sasaki, Xof Xero, Fumiko Ito and Enji Takao, my intelligent unit knows all your abilities, I will create something that can counter this so do not worry, the war will be different than whatever you are thinking" said Looner.

A shadow appears where Rain and Looner are standing, they begin to fall into the shadows.

"I will see you soon Izanagi," said Rain.

Izanagi brings Kori, Silva, and David back to the academy.

"Kori, go and get checked out with the medical team, we will need you to recover for when the war is here" Izanagi instructed.

"Yes Sensei".

Izanagi heads to Ichiro's office, he is joined by all the grand Loch Warriors.

"Rain, we should have destroyed him back in the day, that would have stopped the Dark Kingdom in their tracks," said Ichiro.

"So, Rain is the leader of the Dark Kingdom, that bastard," said Enji.

"Yes, he said the war will commence one month today, when he said the outskirts of the Loch Kingdom, I think he means the huge desert area" Izanagi explains.

"How strong would five thousand men with magical energy be?" Fumiko wondered.

"The Dark Kingdom has weak men; I alone will destroy them all" said Xof.

"We will use all of our Loch Warriors, the first years and be at the back and only assist the higher grades, we need a meeting with the king, he may be able to spare some of his army to assist long range," said Izanagi.

"Agreed, I will arrange a meeting with him, we must prepare all Loch Warriors, Grand Loch Warriors are in charge, grade three and two will be in charge of large groups of Loch Warriors," said Ichiro.

"Yes Sir!!" they said together.

Ichiro

19 – War Announcement

Kori is fully healed by Erika, Loch Warrior academies greatest magical healer. Kori analysed how she healed and saw that she used her magical energy to connect to the natural aspects of magical energy. He leaves the medical area and walks back to his dorm room; he sits on his bed and feels frustrated.

"How can I be so below the dark kingdom, Rain's magic was way out of my league, maybe Okifumi is the reason why I have gotten so far".

Kori heads to sleep, he feels useless and thinks he would be no help in the upcoming war.

The morning was bright, the sun shined through Kori's window, he wakes up and gets ready. As he puts on his blue jacket, he hears a voice on a speaker in the corner of his room.

"Wakey, wakey everyone, I am your glorious sensei Izanagi, please can all loch warriors meet me in the courtyard in fifteen minutes, thank you".

"He must be announcing the war against the dark kingdom" Kori thought.

Kori heads outside and sees Luna and Kaito walking down the path.

"Hey guys wait up!!" Kori shouts.

"Oh, hey Kori, how are your injuries?" Luna asked.

"All healed up, bout yourself?".

"I am all healed thanks".

"I wonder why Izanagi sensei wants to see everyone, could it be about you, David and Silva being taken to the dark kingdom's base" Kaito wondered.

"Yeah, the leader of the dark kingdom is declaring war on Loch".

"Huh, that's crazy a full-on war with the dark kingdom" Kaito looked worried.

They reach the courtyard and all loch warriors of every year and grade are waiting by the podium. Kori sees Namiyo and heads over to greet him.

"Hey Namiyo sensei".

"Oh Kori, how have you been?".

"Not bad, did you see me in the tournament?".

"Well for what was the tournament, yeah you was very impressive, you might have a bigger potential than me, but it is too soon to tell kid".

"Thanks Namiyo Sensei, one day when I release Shinka, you will be that shocked you just give me your title of Grade 3" said Kori, he smiles.

"Good one kid, now let's listen to Izanagi Sensei's announcement".

"Welcome all, it is I the great Izanagi, I have important news I must share with you all!!".

"Izanagi Sensei is always full of himself" Silva thought.

"The Dark Kingdom has declared war upon us all, most importantly in a month they will march upon Loch Kingdom, we will not allow that, each one of you will fight in the war and we will put an end to the Dark Kingdom, as Loch Warriors it is our duty to protect everyone in Loch and that is what we will do, now train, prepare, make sure you are ready because we will show the Dark Kingdom why Loch is not a country to be messed with!!".

Everyone cheers on Izanagi's speech and are pumped and ready to fight for Loch, Kori looks up with a sad face, he feels something strange within himself.

"I need to get stronger; I need to find out more about this Okifumi thing inside me" he thought.

"**I can hear you, little brat, what do you want to know?**".

"How are you inside me?" Kori asked.

"**I am not inside you; I am connected to your soul, I do not know exactly how I am connected, my soul was sealed into a dimension and when you was born my soul reverted to your soul**".

"I see, very strange, well if you are going to be a part of my life then I need you to help me unlock your powers as well".

"**Are you trying to bargain with me?**".

"You can call it that, if I die then surely your soul will just cease to exist".

"So, you are not entirely dumb, I will make you a deal, I will help you understand my powers if you promise to find a way after the war to split our souls".

"Okay deal, as long as you are not evil".

"I used to be just like you, a guy with dreams, but they were taken away from me, so you do not have to worry about me being evil".

"Okay, let's do some training right away, thank you Okifumi".

Somewhere in the West corner of Loch, men in dark cloaks lurk. Rain and Looner enter Folklore Village, it is the home of the witches. Rain smirks as Evelyn Evergrande walks down the steps from her keep.

"Thank you for having us," said Rain.

"Remember Rain, I have only allowed you passage into Loch without the kingdom knowing because I want to see the downfall of the Loch Warriors, you better hold your promise," said Evelyn.

"Do not worry my Evelyn, I have created a warrior on par with Izanagi, this war will be our win".

Rain and the others enter Evelyn's keep, ready for war preparations.

Back at the Loch Academy, the Grand Loch Warriors begin intense training with all the Loch Warriors. Izanagi walks up to a tired Silva with his hands on his hips.

"Silva, have you seen Kori? He has not turned up to training today" he asked.

"No Sensei, he was talking to himself in the hallway this morning, I think he is finally going crazy".

"I see, how strange".

"Maybe the soul inside him is finally communicating with him, not sure if this is bad or a good thing" Izanagi thought.

Kori is sat meditating next to a lake located outside the academy, he is focusing his inner magical energy trying to convert both his and Okifumi's magic.

"I feel amazing" he thought.

"Magic is like a natural resource, learning to control it will be key, once this is achieved, I will teach you how to fuse blood magic with your other magical elements".

"I see, I am beginning to understand now".

To be continued in volume 2, the Kingdom war arc....

Loch Warrior Rankings

Ichiro Kido – Head Loch Warrior
Izanagi Sasaki – Grand Loch Warrior
Fumiko Ito – Grand Loch Warrior
Xof Xero – Grand Loch Warrior
Enji Takao – Grand Loch Warrior
Atticus – Grand Loch Warrior
Namiyo - Rank 3 Loch Warrior

Kori and others are all Loch Warriors in training.

Printed in Great Britain
by Amazon